By

TREGARTHUR'S
PROMISE

Alex Mellanby

Cillian Press |

First published in Great Britain in 2013
by Cillian Press Limited. 83 Ducie Street, Manchester M1 2JQ
www.cillianpress.co.uk

British Library Cataloguing in Publication Data.
A catalogue record for this book is available from the British Library.

Paperback ISBN: 978-0-9573155-4-9
eBook ISBN: 978-0-9573155-5-6

Cover Design: Billie Jade McNeill
Photography: Niels Mickers

Published by
Cillian Press – Manchester - 2013
www.cillianpress.co.uk

This book is dedicated to Pat Read who has safely led so many expeditions across Dartmoor and to the many who have faced the Ten Tors challenge.

CONTENTS

LOST ON THE MOOR.......7

THE CAVE.......17

FOOD.......27

ANOTHER DAY.......48

THE NOTE.......56

CONFRONTATION.......73

A VISITOR.......83

BREAK-UP.......94

RYAN'S STORY.......102

EXPEDITION.......109

TIGER CAVE.......116

CROW.......130

THE HUNT.......142

THE PROMISE.......149

TRAPPED.......153

BURIAL.......167

RE-UNITED.......171

WINTER.......181

SPRING.......195

INTO THE BLUE.......201

MISS TREGARTHUR.......214

LOST ON THE MOOR

One advantage of having a drug dealing family with a reputation for extreme violence is that you get left alone at school. There are disadvantages, several disadvantages, and they had all mixed together into one big mess. That was the reason I was on a bus – a school trip. I needed to get away, a quiet time to think.

'Off!' A piercing screech crashed into my thoughts. I looked up to see Demelza Honey – the queen of slap and supposed school beauty – march down the aisle and take over the back seat with her followers. There was only just enough space for their overstuffed makeup bags.

Not far behind, the wiry little rat face of Zach Bishop appeared. 'Move!' he shouted and poked someone sitting in the seat he wanted, pulling the boy to the ground and kicking him before slumping down, sticking his feet into the aisle and telling his two slimy hangers-on to sit opposite.

This trip wasn't a good idea – whatever it was. Someone had mixed the bad and dangerous with the small and weak, school leavers and some from the junior school. This wasn't a dream, someone had nightmared this one up. Peace and quiet? No chance.

'Alvin, you came.' Big Jen – Jenna Karen – squashed into the seat beside me and pointing backwards: 'What are they doing here?' But Jenna could see I didn't have answers. She went on: 'Things at home just as bad then.' That wasn't a question. Jenna knew. Her family were on the same road.

A teacher got on, she looked wild – eyes that almost popped out of her head when she talked, and dressed in army gear with enough kit for a year long expedition. Wild and a bit familiar. Miss Tregarthur, the trip sheet said. I think she taught at the junior school, but I recognised her from somewhere else. She stared down the row of seats. I was sure I'd seen her around our house, talking to my aunt. That set me worrying.

I didn't want to think about home right now so I actually listened to the roll call, the instructions. The teacher told us about the other two mothers who were there to help, they were weird too – they looked like twins with the same hair problems. The three of them sat down and let the mayhem continue. Stuff was flying in the air – boots, coats, and cuddly toys from the smaller kids. The bus moved off.

Outside we passed woods and fields, quiet and peaceful. Inside Zach was torturing those smaller kids and Demelza was trying new shades of eyeliner on reluctant volunteers.

The teacher looked asleep. Leave them alone, I thought and made myself look out of the window. A couple of hours passed before we pulled up, piled out, and this Joint Venture school walking trip walked off, with most in a rush to get away from trouble. Some hope.

We walked.

'Where are we?' I looked hopefully at Jenna. I could see hills rolling away into the distance, but no houses. It didn't look like anywhere I wanted to be. 'It's a huge nothing.'

Jenna didn't answer. She looked as worried as me.

'Dartmoor Park,' started Miss Tregarthur, swinging into full lecture mode. 'The largest area of granite ...'

I switched off. She was going on about wild stuff. It certainly looked wild. Miss Tregarthur led, not looking back. Her two helpers lagged behind.

At first, wherever we were, looked like it was straight out of a nature film – warm sunlight, a sparkling stream bordering the path, sheep grazing in the distance. Zach pushed most of the younger ones into the water. I stuck to higher ground just in case. I wasn't looking for a fight, yet. The bus journey had brought back all my other worries. Only a few more weeks until I was sixteen, only a few more weeks before they threw me out.

We walked some more and then even more. I looked up to the hills. Huge grey stones stood out on their tops.

'Must be the granite,' Jen muttered. Perhaps she'd been listening more closely to the teacher.

We stopped to eat; packs had been handed out on the bus. Zach and his groupie pair made lunch painful for many. I lost count of the times Jenna told me: 'Leave them, it's not worth it.' I couldn't understand why they were annoying me. Sorting them seemed so much easier than sorting my life.

Off we went again. The path became steeper as we left the stream. It wasn't easy and the group spread out. Soon we were picking our way over rocks, climbing towards one of the peaks.

'Didn't know this was a rock climbing trip,' muttered Jenna.

'Looks worse further up,' I peered ahead – huge boulders

seemed to be closing in around us.

A breeze started. Weather here changed fast. The wind grew stronger, rolling in the clouds and hiding the sun. I pulled my fleece tighter. Higher up the boulders were as big as houses, looming over the path. The sky became a nasty threatening grey. A few watery drops fell in the wind.

Miss Tregarthur waved us on. 'Only a bit of rain. Don't stop. Nothing unusual. But hurry up.' There was something rather like panic in her voice.

The rain fell harder, huge paintball size drops splattered on the ground. The air was soon thick with wet cloud.

No one hurried, just more pushing and shoving. The teacher had no idea how to control this lot. She took another look at the dark clouds. Then her shouting started: 'Get up that hill! Run.' And now shrieking: 'Run! Run! Run!' but it was too late, even if anyone had taken any notice of her. Rain pelted down and the wind blew her shouts away.

If rain wasn't unusual I knew it wasn't normal when the ground started shaking. Someone screamed, 'Earthquake!'

I might never have been on the moor or on a school hiking trip before, but when the huge boulders crashed down the hillside like giant beasts coming out of the gathering mist I knew this was even worse than Zach and the rest of them. Death looked more than likely.

I ran through blinding rain, but rocks seemed to be everywhere in my way and seconds later I crashed into a cliff wall I was sure hadn't been there before. I felt my way along the rock face and tripped, tumbling into a gap and sliding down into darkness. Scrambling to my feet I saw I was in a cave stretching in front of me into the hillside. Dark and gloomy but in the distance a faint blue light radiated out of the dark. I could hear sounds of the storm outside. In the cave it was still and quiet, almost as though the earthquake, or whatever it was, didn't exist.

I turned, climbed back up, and looked for the others. For a second, the wind cleared the cloud of mist. I saw Miss Tregarthur further up the hill. A giant slab of stone had fallen across her, pinning her to the ground. She struggled frantically, unable to escape, screaming. But she wasn't screaming for help. A gust of wind carried her strange words: 'Keep my promise. Keep it. Save him.' More rocks fell on her. A swirl of cloud curled down the hillside, she started to disappear, then she looked up. Almost as though she was searching me out. Her face twisted in a hideous snarl as she howled: 'YOU – Alvin Carter – YOU – keep my promise.' That was the last I saw of her.

I had no idea what she meant, it made no sense and I didn't much care. I was thinking about survival. There was nowhere out there to run, nowhere safe. Disappearing into the cave felt safer.

The cloud cleared again. I saw the others – mud soaked, lashed by the wind and rain – they were trying to get down the hill. But the way seemed blocked as though the stones of the moor had moved to trap them. Torrents of water washed down the path. I looked away. What did I care? Then I heard Jenna's calls for help. Peering back I shouted, 'Over here! Over here!' again and again, and waved my arms.

Jenna made it but she wasn't alone. When I saw the others I wished I hadn't bothered: that spoilt bitch Demelza and ... surely not ... Zach. But they were just part of the group, difficult to tell how many in that chaos.

We all slid down into the cave, crowding around the entrance, but the driving rain soon pushed us further into the gloom.

In the next second everything seemed to stop outside. The wind died. All became still and silent. I looked again at the back of the cave and now I could make out a narrow tunnel, the entrance lit by the faint blue haze of light. A damp rotten smell hung in the air. The still quiet wasn't right. I knew something bad was about to happen. I was good at that sort of prediction, bad things often happened around me.

A deep rumbling started. It came from way out on the moor, growing louder and louder until a thundering wave of noise rushed towards us. The ground shook and cracked under my feet. Sounds of the earth breaking filled the cave. Demelza screamed the loudest as rocks smashed down over the entrance. We couldn't stay here and we couldn't get out.

I went for the tunnel, yelling: 'This way.'

'What? In there? No way!' Jenna yelled back, seeing the dimly lit narrow passage.

There was no time to argue. Huge rocks fell into the cave entrance, rolling down towards us. Everyone pressed towards me, moving into the tunnel, onwards into air thick with dust and fear. I felt my way forward in the faint blue light. The rest were still pushing against me. There was no way back – the entrance now completely blocked.

'Quick.' 'Help.' 'Move!' came the shouts from behind me.

Voices echoed against the stone walls.

'What about that teacher?' someone called.

'She's had it, I think.'

'Shouldn't we go back for her?'

'Can't,' I shouted. 'And if we hang on we'll all die. Come on.'

Nobody went back. The blue light grew stronger, always just ahead of us, as though showing the way. I stood to one side as some of the others pushed past. Then I heard more stones crashing down. The tunnel roof was crumbling behind us.

'Move it!' I was pushing with the rest.

One of the younger ones fell to his knees shaking and whimpering. Someone grabbed the fallen figure and pushed him forward. I couldn't see who had helped but he looked bigger than most of the others.

Then I heard more shouts: 'Get out of the way.' Zach barged through. I thought of tripping him up but in the end I just moved aside, waiting for Jenna. She appeared, pushing, shoving and half-carrying two smaller children. I liked Jen but I never thought of her as a caring sort of person. She tripped over Demelza who had slipped and lay moaning.

'Get up.' Jenna seized Demelza's arm, wrenched her to her feet and shoved her hard. Grabbing the two other children again Jenna pushed onwards.

Another boy kept stopping and looking back as though expecting Miss Tregarthur to reappear. She didn't. His scream echoed in the tunnel. I turned and saw the boy's leg pinned underneath a massive lump of fallen stone. If Jenna was helping, maybe I should too. I turned back and tried to lift the rock but I couldn't do it on my own.

'Help, back here!' I yelled. 'Where's that big bloke? Help.'

A shape appeared through the dust. Together we heaved. The boy screamed and passed out but we'd moved the rock enough for me to drag him clear. We carried his unconscious body onwards.

The tunnel ended, the blue light disappeared and in a rush we stumbled out. Daylight was fading. Behind us the rumbling and crashing continued. Everyone was spluttering and coughing, wiping away the dirt from their faces. We lowered the injured boy onto some grass outside the entrance. The rest collapsed on the ground, picking places between the rocks.

'Is he still alive?' asked Jenna.

The boy groaned.

'Seems so.' I turned to see if anyone else had followed us in the tunnel; there was no one.

The sounds of the earthquake stopped again, leaving an empty silence. Looking around it felt like something from history – an old war picture in black, white and mud. People slumped on the grass, some shivering even though it wasn't cold. No one talked, no one stirred, nothing happened. We hadn't moved far from the end of the tunnel. It was too dark to move about safely.

'What do we do?' Jenna stood and was silhouetted against the last of the light.

She seemed to be speaking to me – I had no idea.

'I suppose we wait until they find us,' someone said.

'Don't think they will,' a girl's voice came from back in the tunnel, her voice miserable enough to spark off even more crying.

'Of course they'll find us, they have rescue teams.' Another girl sounded just as uncertain and other voices started up.

'What happened to the others?'

'Left behind.'

'Did you see the teacher?'

'I think she got hit by a rock.'

'If they're all dead then no one will know to come after us.'

'They're not all dead. Some must have gone back.'

'Why don't our phones work?'

All our mobile phones were blank: no signal, no power. Dead no matter how much poking, all dead.

It started to rain again. I could just see that we were at the top of a slope. Behind me the tunnel came out from a huge cliff. I couldn't see any way to get out of here. Nothing felt right. At the bottom of the slope it looked as though there might be a forest. I saw shapes moving in the wind. Rustling and scuffling noises came from the trees, but nothing else. There were no lights, no sounds of cars or people.

The injured boy let out another groan. His leg was still bleeding.

'Let me help.' One of the girls moved towards him.

I'd almost felt it was my job to do something, as though leading them all through the tunnel meant I was responsible. I didn't like that thought and I had no idea what to do. Better that someone else should do it. The girl tried to look at the wound and I heard another painful moan.

'I can't see. It's too dark,' she said to Jenna, who had joined her. 'I need to tie something over the wound.'

I knew the girl who'd helped – Mary – everyone called her 'Nurse Mary' even before this walk. She'd always talked about becoming a nurse like her mother. Did she know what she was doing with a real emergency? Mary took off her jacket and tied the sleeves tightly across the wound, a strange bandage. The injured boy shrieked with pain but the bleeding seemed to stop.

'Help me move him.' Mary looked over at me but I turned away. She let out an angry sigh and I felt my face burn. Why me? I'd done my bit, someone else could help.

The rain fell harder. The tunnel provided the only shelter and we all moved back under cover. Inside the opening it seemed as though there was another cave, much larger by the sounds of our echoing voices, but it was impossible to make out any details.

We waited. Sometimes we could hear rocks falling. There was still no sign of rescue. Night came. I don't know what I expected to happen – sirens and the sounds of emergency teams perhaps – but there was nothing; mostly just a deep silence, but occasionally the noise of something moving outside. Someone would shout: 'Who's there?' but no one answered. And no one was going out to look around.

Finally I stretched out on the cave floor. A dim moon gave the only light; a darkness blacker than I'd ever known. I pulled my jacket over my head, trying to keep out the sobbing, moaning, and constant unanswerable questions. It didn't work.

'What happens if the roof falls in?' whined one of the younger children. I soon came to recognise that whine.

'You get buried alive.'

And I did recognise that voice – Zach. Everyone recognised Zach's voice.

During the long night on the stony cave floor Zach continued to make fake animal noises, shouting, 'What was that?'

Then a far louder howl seemed to answer Zach's pathetic call, and screeching wails echoed round the cave. Someone started screaming and others joined in. I wanted them to shut up in case whatever was howling heard the noise. I wanted to tell them to shut up, but I couldn't find my voice. Mary, treading with care in the dark, moved over to those whimpering the loudest and tried to comfort them. The sounds outside the cave fell quiet again in the deep night.

Nothing made sense. Had we been abandoned? I'd led us out of the earthquake, or whatever had happened. It wouldn't be long before they blamed me if no one came to rescue us.

The night passed slowly.

-2-

THE CAVE

I gave up trying to sleep. Rocks on the cave floor jabbed my every move. Restless bodies sprawled around me, more restless in the first signs of light in a strange grey dawn. I looked out. Sounds had started up – squawking birds mixed with grunts and more scuffling. Nothing sounded like the noises we'd heard yesterday on the moor, nothing sounded friendly.

And it didn't look like the place we had left. Even in daylight I couldn't make sense of it. The tunnel had ended in another large cave with a roof stretching up above me. The floor was a mess of sand and fallen stone, mostly dry, but gloomy and dark. I moved outside and sat on a rock.

'Where are we?' Jenna squashed down beside me. She wasn't a small girl and it was good to have the warmth of someone next to me.

'No idea.' I worried that she expected me to know.

'No way up there.' She pointed at the cliff behind us. It seemed endless in all directions. 'And I don't like the look of anything down there either.'

Below our cave it looked as though a rock fall might have cleared the slope down to the forest. The ground was strewn with broken trees and bushes.

'Do you know anything about that teacher?' I asked. I didn't want to talk about the scenery. The forest was just trees going on forever and I didn't like it.

'Eh?'

'Have you ever seen her before this trip?'

Jenna gave me a growl. 'No, she joined the Junior school last term. Don't know anything else about her, don't want to know anything about her. What do you mean?'

'Nothing. I think she got crushed in the earthquake.' Why had she been shouting at me? Her twisted face stuck in my thoughts. How did she know my name? What had she meant by keeping her promise?

'Did you hear her shouting?' I said.

'Shouting? No. I heard a lot of screaming. I think it was Jack saying we should go back for her.'

'Jack?'

'The one who hurt his leg. He's in our year isn't he?' Jenna gave me one of her looks. We shared quite a lot, but I'd not spent much time in school recently.

'Lucky what's his name was there, otherwise Jack would still be stuck under that stone.'

'Big Matt you mean, nice guy, bit slow.'

Jenna stood and took a step back towards the cave, watching the others. I didn't want her to go.

'So you didn't hear that teacher going on about some promise?' I blurted out.

'What? No. What do you mean?' Jenna turned and gave me a very suspicious look.

I tried to laugh. 'Nothing, I just thought I heard her say something.'

'What?' Jenna had on her fierce face.

'I'm not sure. She was really frantic. I just caught her eyes. Like she was looking for me. She seemed to be shouting something about keeping her promise and saving someone.'

'What are you on about? Sounds weird. Have you been taking something?'

'No, you know I don't. I may live with it but I'm not stupid. You didn't have to ask.' I was angry that she'd asked about drugs even though she was right that I had sounded weird.

'Sorry. Anyway it's too late to find out now what she meant.' Jenna looked as though she wanted to get away from me.

I glanced up at her face. She often tried to frown, but it didn't always work. Jenna caught me staring and looked back with a, 'What?' I turned away, just catching the hint of one of her rare smiles.

I changed direction: 'Home just as bad?'

Jenna's head fell forward. She took a while before saying anything. 'I just can't get through to Mum. She's got it into her head that it's Ok to keep changing boyfriends – or step-dads as she wants me to call them.'

'Nice.' It was the wrong thing to say.

'NICE? Not nice at all. When they've had enough of Mum they seem to think I'm the next best thing.'

This time I didn't say anything, just waited. I thought she was going to give me the full on Jenna glare but there was no anger in her look now. She seemed near to breakdown.

'She even stopped me putting a lock on my bedroom door.'

And with that she walked away. I could understand why she was always angry back at school. But in the earthquake she'd seemed a different person – helping.

I sat still, watching the rest, thinking about Jenna. Zach

tried to swagger out of the cave, as always with his two creepy followers, and then Demelza with her own hangers-on. Rescue better come quick or there would be murder in the air.

As the light grew stronger some of the others moved on to the patchy grass near to the cave. I didn't know how many had come through the tunnel. Looking back at the group I made it fourteen including me, but they kept moving around, maybe it was more.

'This place doesn't smell right either,' said one of the younger girls who I think had been listening to my conversation with Jenna.

A stale rotten stench came up from the forest of trees, blown on a wind carrying gusts of drizzle along with the smell. Damp and a summer cool.

'Where is everyone? How long is it going to be before they come and get us? What do we do now?' Demelza was practically stamping her feet.

I could think of several things she could do, all painful, although she was saying what I guess we all thought. To me this place looked like real trouble, maybe even worse than the trouble I had at home.

'What are those? They don't look real.' One of Demelza's followers pointed to the gigantic plants that became clearer, trees with enormous branches reaching out in twisted shapes, covered with long trailing creepers. New noises started.

'Sounds like the zoo,' said one of the two girls still staying near to Jenna. 'One of those big cages full of birds.'

Then a wild roar echoed against the cliff followed by grunts and howls. Squeals and cries came from our group. The two girls clung round Jenna's neck. Roars and grunts grew louder and louder, ending with a screaming wail. I thought something was coming towards us. A dark shape moved in the bushes but nothing appeared. Jenna pushed the girls away.

Demelza stood over me. 'Where are we? Why hasn't anyone come to help?'

I ignored her and turned away.

'Well? You got us here.' And she poked me.

'How should I know?' I really didn't want a conversation with Demelza and I didn't want poking either, so I prodded her back rather hard. She slipped and sprawled on the ground, looked up with her mouth open and hate on her face.

'When are we going to go home?' the whining boy whined.

'Shut up Stevie,' hushed one of the others from the junior school.

If that boy didn't shut up himself then I thought someone would do it for him.

'I'm hungry.' Stevie could moan as well as whine.

The girl who had told him to keep quiet gave him a piece of chocolate she'd saved. No one had much left from the lunch we'd been given on the walk. We were all hungry.

'What you got then?' Zach stood over one of the younger girls. She froze.

'Back off Zach,' Jenna snarled at him.

Zach moved away with a stupid grin pretending to make it a joke. His face twisted and he spat some words that I didn't hear. I looked at Jen, there was something strange about her. Almost as though coming through that tunnel had made her different, or was that just normal? Zach wasn't going to have it all his own way.

Checking my own pack I found I'd not really eaten much

the day before so I handed a sandwich to Jen.

'Thanks, maybe I should give it ...' she looked around at the younger kids, but thought again and bit into it. 'Thanks,' she mumbled again.

Jack had been keeping quiet, but as he moved to get at his pack he groaned and held his leg.

'Let me look.' Mary knelt down beside him.

Mary was doing her best to keep up the nursing. I watched, everybody watched, as she gently untied the jacket she had used to bandage the injury. The blood soaked cloth stuck to the wound and Jack flinched, tears in his eyes. As she pulled the jacket away, the bleeding started again.

'We need some sort of dressing,' Mary said to Jenna in a hushed voice.

'I've got a spare T-shirt,' someone offered.

Mary tore the shirt and wrapped the cloth around the wound using strips of the material to tie it in place.

'I should have cleaned it,' Mary said looking at Jack's leg. 'But ... someone will come soon and rescue us ... they'll bring a medical team ... at least the T-shirt won't stick to the wound ... like the wool did from my jacket ...' Mary shut up as she saw everyone looking at her, listening to her anxious chatter.

'Thanks,' Jack mumbled.

A strange looking girl came slowly out from the back of the cave. I'd missed her in my count. She had always been a loner; I can't remember ever talking to her at school. Her tall, thin body was usually dressed in homemade black clothes, odd, and so miserable. 'There's no one here to save us.' Her slow, sad, hopeless cry echoed against the dripping stones. 'We're all going to die – eaten by that roaring thing.'

Her words started the sobbing off again.

'That's rubbish. Ivy, you always say miserable things. Someone will find us soon … won't they?' I heard so much uncertainty in Mary's voice.

'It's like the Lost World … you know … like that old film, isn't it?' Another boy pointed towards the forest and the mountains that now became visible in the far distance.

'Sam! Where did you come from?' He'd appeared behind Mary and startled her.

I hadn't seen Sam before either. 'Are there any more in there?' I pointed into the darkness of the cave.

'No. It was just me and Ivy,' said Sam.

I knew Sam. He was a small fat boy with a round face which made him look younger than the rest of us in our year. Sam always seemed to be trying not to get noticed and somehow always failed. He needed to keep out of Zach's way.

Yesterday I overheard a conversation between the hair-problem mothers on the bus talking about Sam. It had almost made me forget my own problems. One of them had said something about Sam's dad dying in a car crash and, 'Yes and no mother either,' the other had replied. I hadn't heard the rest.

'Lost world – that means real monsters.' Zach moved up close to Sam, roared in his ear and smacked him hard on the head.

'Shut it Zach,' said Jenna.

'You again, what's up with you?' Zach sounded genuinely surprised.

'I'm tired and fed up with you going on.' Her words met silence.

'You want to try and shut me up then?' Zach squared up to Jenna.

Jenna stood her ground and stared back at him. Jen might be

a big girl, but with Zach and the other two she didn't have much of a chance. Somehow I found myself standing next to her. It was enough. Zach turned away, confused, but with something much worse in his eyes. Everyone else must have been holding their breath and now it seemed that they all breathed out at the same time.

'I wonder what happened to the rest of them on the walk,' Jack said. 'There were a lot more of us when we started out.'

'At least they're not stuck in this stinking cave.' Zach looked at me.

'Probably all dead,' muttered Ivy.

''Bout time Alvin came up with a plan.' Zach pointed at me. 'You got us stuck here. Now do something about it.'

Backing down had got to Zach; it wouldn't be long before this came to more than words. I wasn't that hard, I didn't have to be – I relied on my family's reputation. They weren't here, but it wasn't the thought of fighting Zach that worried me. I wondered why I had led the way yesterday. Had it really been my decision? It felt more like the falling rocks had chased us down the tunnel.

'If Alvin hadn't got us out of the earthquake we'd all be dead.' Jenna seemed determined to antagonise Zach.

'Might be best if we were,' said Ivy.

I needed to do something. Had that teacher's screams only been aimed at me? Had she singled me out or was that my imagination? I needed to find out if anyone else had heard her. Not now though – now I needed a plan.

'Has anyone looked at the tunnel?' There was no reply so I walked into the dark at the back of the cave. Everyone else followed.

Even in the dim daylight I could see the huge boulders piled up, closing off any hope of escape. I pushed at the stones and kicked them, nothing happened.

'Is there anyone there?' Mary shouted at the wall of rocks and everyone joined in: 'Hello ...' 'Help ... can you hear me?' 'Get us out of here!'

We stood back, listening. No sounds came from the other side of the rock pile, only echoes on ours. We tried again and again, hammering on the rocks with bits of stone.

'Great idea Alvin,' muttered Zach and jabbed his finger at me. I caught it, held on while our eyes met. Zach snatched his hand back and sneered at me. But my idea had been useless. I moved away. That was the last time I was going to make a suggestion.

From time to time one or two went back and banged on the rocks blocking the tunnel and called out. No response.

'Do you think we should go looking for help?' Mary said.

'What, down there?' Jenna pointed at the forest as the sounds we'd heard in the night started again.

'We have to stay here ... don't we? Otherwise they won't be able to find us.' Jack sounded desperate.

'Jack's right,' Mary said. 'We should stay here.'

Jack was stuck here and Mary seemed so keen on agreeing with him. I felt that Jen was right. There was nothing down in the forest that looked hopeful. Or safe.

The day went on and on, just expecting someone to arrive, some sound of people. You don't go for a walk and everyone vanishes. What had happened? What did we need to do?

There were lots of useless suggestions. Nobody did anything. Demelza kept going on, saying someone should go down into the forest – but not her. I could see they were looking to someone to lead. There wasn't anyone. Even Zach was quiet and I wasn't going to do anything. The teacher's words and her face kept coming back to me. Surely what she said meant there had to be someone here? I thought we should wait. If we wandered off then nobody would find us. Since no one did anything and no one went anywhere, the day just passed away and the light started to fade again.

None of us were going anywhere in the dark. Zach had been right – I didn't have any idea what to do. It had been stupid to think I could do anything. I tried to sleep, an empty stomach made that difficult. I suppose we were all starting to think that there might be no rescue. Tomorrow we were going to have to do something for ourselves.

-3-

FOOD

My sleep ended in another grey dawn. Jenna was already standing at the cave entrance.

'Where are they?' I heard her whisper. 'Where are we?'

I tapped her on the shoulder and she jumped. 'Talking to yourself?'

'No one else,' Jenna replied.

A sound from Jack made us turn. He sat rocking backwards and forwards, holding his injured leg. He looked up. 'Anything? Any sign of anyone?'

'Nothing,' said Jenna.

My thoughts couldn't leave the teacher's screaming words. What could they mean? We all needed saving but I couldn't see anyone special in our group. Had anyone else heard her, made sense of her words?

'Jack, you looked like you were waiting for that teacher. Did you see her?' I asked.

'Thought I saw her get hit by a rock or something.' Jack winced as he spoke.

'Did you hear her say anything?'

'No. Like what?'

'Nothing.' Maybe it had been a hallucination, I'd dreamt up the words.

The rest were waking, stretching and groaning. They looked a mess – particularly the group from the junior school. They'd tried to look after each other. Scared of anyone from the senior school. I thought only four of them had made it through the tunnel, three girls and the boy who whined – Stevie. Two of the girls were called Sara and there didn't seem much difference between them. Both were rather small and freckly. One was blond and the other a bit more ginger. Both looked miserable.

'Nothing is going to happen, we're all going to starve to death,' said the gingery Sara. 'And I want a wee, but everyone's watching and I'm too scared to go down there.' She pointed towards the trees, but stopped with her mouth open, noticing everyone listening to her. She pulled her jacket over her face.

In the dark, there were several large boulders to crouch behind. But in the light it wasn't so easy. The cave had started to smell. Sara was right – everyone watched if anyone moved.

Jenna gave out an angry sigh, walked over to Sara, took her hand and led her out of the cave. The rest watched. Jenna stopped and turned, hands on her hips, and glared.

'What?!' she yelled and everyone looked away. The two of them headed for the nearest bushes.

I wondered if she would bring Sara back, the old Jenna probably wouldn't, but here? I didn't know. Getting away from home seemed to have changed her.

Sara's words about starving sounded about right. I must have been muttering about getting food because Jack looked at me and said, 'How?'

I stared back at him. I wasn't going to make any more suggestions, not that I had any.

'Suppose we'll have to go and look,' Jack went on. 'Might be something we can eat down in the forest.'

'Like what?'

Jack shrugged. 'Do you think they'll find us today?' and he looked down at his leg.

'Not sure who you mean.' I was thinking that the noises might mean anything could find us and might be looking for food as well.

Jack didn't seem to pick up what I meant. 'Rescuers, police, someone on the moor. They have teams that rescue people.' He tried to be cheerful.

I was out of cheerfulness. 'We're not on the moor. No idea where we are or who is around. There's nothing out there.'

'Won't they break through the tunnel?'

'Maybe.' It didn't seem likely to me so I moved away from Jack in case he asked more questions.

Today the sun burnt off the mist hanging over the forest and the sky cleared. Jenna did return with Sara. If Jenna could go wandering about then so could I. I left the cave and walked along the cliff; staring upwards I still couldn't see the top. The slimy stone was far too steep to climb.

Cascades of water tumbled down the rock face and splashed onto the ground. One cascade poured into a hollow, creating a small pool. I bent down, scooped some of the water into my hand and tasted it with the tip of my tongue. It seemed alright, but what would poison water taste like? Thirst stopped me worrying for long. I just drank and drank. The rest had been watching and seeing that I didn't drop dead they ran to the small pool.

'Is it safe?' Mary asked. I gave her the 'no idea' look. Mary drank.

It was a fight. There wasn't enough room, everyone scrabbled to get to the pool, jostling for space, driven by a day of having little to drink other than what they had left in their water bottles from the walk. I stood back watching them. How long would we survive without help, without any equipment and no food? Watching the pushing and shoving to get to the water, I knew it would soon turn to punches; Zach wasn't the only one who would cause trouble.

I moved off and walked along the bottom of the cliff as it curved away from the cave. The ground sloped upwards and after a while I could hear crashing water. Rounding a corner I saw a huge waterfall, with spray making rainbow colours in the sunlight. Thick plants and trees hid the bottom of the waterfall, but there was a river which looped around the forest below the cave. Several others had followed me.

'I think we're cut off by that river.' Sam stretched his arm and pointed.

'That might keep us safe from whatever made those noises,' said Stevie the whining boy.

'Unless they're on this side.' I couldn't see why I should make things sound better than they were, but it just made Stevie add whimpering to his selection of noises.

Worse still, something slithered off into the bushes. Everyone jumped back. Wherever we were this place wasn't safe.

'Snakes,' muttered Matt, who didn't seem to mind. Jenna gave him a look and held a finger to her lips. I didn't think it was worth pretending. If we were going to stay alive we all needed to know about the danger.

'What are we going to eat?' Jenna said and I thought she was trying to keep off the subject of snakes. 'We've nothing left and it doesn't look like anyone is coming to rescue us.'

'Maybe we can find something in the woods – berries or fruit,' suggested Mary.

'Poisonous,' said Ivy.

You've got to love Ivy. She's so consistent.

'We have to find something,' I said, even though I knew Ivy was right and it would be difficult to know whether anything was safe to eat.

'The noises in the night must mean that there are animals nearby. We'll have to eat them if nothing else happens,' Sam suggested.

'You're joking.' Jenna poked Sam in the chest. He turned red and didn't say more.

'I think I'd rather starve to death than go looking for the thing that roared in the night,' came another whine.

'Of course you aren't going to starve.' Zach was the last to leave the water pool having driven everyone else away. 'I'm going to eat you!' he stepped towards Stevie who screwed his fists into his eyes and bawled.

Zach was really getting to me. At school I just let him get on with bullying and making things awful for anyone weaker than him, although he still kept his two followers just in case. I'd had other things on my mind. I didn't care what he did so long as he stayed away from me – which he did because he'd once met my older brother, who had talked about ripping off his legs. Now he was right here in my face. Yesterday he'd almost poked me. Perhaps fighting him would take my mind off feeling hungry. If it came to it I didn't really care if I lost. Jenna might have been able to do the superwoman bit and change into some caring person but that wasn't me, I'm not a bully but I'm not very nice either. My muscles tightened and I eased through the group who were wandering back to the cave.

Then Jenna was at me, 'Alvin … please.'

I shrugged her off but she grabbed my arm and stopped me. The rest were moving away.

'What now?' I said as we stood alone beneath the cliff.

Jenna looked up at me and I saw fear in her face – I could feel my eyes burning, my breath came fast, and every part of me felt ready to fight.

'If you take on Zach you're going to scare everyone,' she said.

'And?' It sounded to me like she meant, if you take on Zach and lose.

'You won't know when to stop. Or his friends will join in. Someone's got to hold this together.'

'And you think it should be me?'

'There's no one else. Look at them. You're the only one who's any good at organising …'

'Yeah, but only if there's something in it for me. That's how our family works. You know that. Something in it or someone gets damaged.' I was pulling away from her.

'I thought you were different.' Jenna looked hurt.

'No chance, no chance to be different.'

'But you weren't like that in the earthquake, not then. If you hadn't done something we'd have all been crushed by rocks.'

I looked at her. Was she right? It hadn't come easy. Should I tell her all the things the teacher said? I thought that would bring me more trouble. Then even Jenna would blame me, saying it was all because of me, something to do with me and that teacher. Was it all because of me anyway, something to do with home? The fighting idea drained away.

Looking at Jenna I felt a grin slowly starting on my face. 'Are you always going to save Zach?'

'Maybe, but why don't you go and try to find something to eat – take Zach with you.'

'You don't ask much. Do I have to bring him back?'

Jenna didn't answer that question. I could read her thoughts. If something happened at least it would be away from the others. I splashed my face with water from the pool and returned to the cave. Zach was still taunting Stevie.

So I tried to do what Jenna wanted. 'Zach, instead of getting at Stevie, why don't we go and see if we can find something else to eat?'

'Eh?' said Zach as though he couldn't believe what he heard.

'That's if you're up to it?'

Zach looked around him. Everyone watched.

'Yeah, we'll go.' Zach tried to sound as though he was up to it but turned to his two followers looking for support. 'You two can come.'

Did I care if there were three of them? Back at school they wouldn't have touched me. Not unless they wanted to end up in hospital. But here there was only me. I turned and raised my eyebrows at Jen. She mouthed 'no problem' at me.

'Should we start a fire?' Jack asked before I left. 'You know, in case there's someone around. They might see the smoke.'

'And how do we do that?' Jenna frowned.

'You rub sticks together or bash bits of stone,' suggested Sam.

'Zach! Any of you lot got a lighter?' I called down to Zach and the other two who had already started slowly down the slope.

'Yep,' shouted one of them and he turned back rather more quickly. 'Can I help light the fire?' he said holding up the lighter.

'Ryan, get back down here,' Zach demanded.

I went down with Ryan. Sam followed, I thought I should have stopped him but he just tagged along. We caught up with Zach at the edge of the forest where he had stopped in front of a tangled mass of dripping green.

'What about snakes?' asked Sam.

'Go find out.' Zach grabbed him and shoved. Sam toppled into the vegetation and yelped. The plants weren't soft and squidgy; they were tough and spiny. Sam stood up digging thorns out of his arm.

'No snakes then,' sneered Zach as he pushed Sam out of the way.

So, whether I cared or not I suppose Zach had done something useful. If there were snakes then sacrificing Sam might not be a bad idea. Next time maybe I'd push Zach. That thought cheered me up quite a lot.

We could only move slowly. It didn't look as though anything had passed this way recently – if ever. We tore branches from the trees and smashed a way through. Zach managed to get me into the lead. The slope flattened out. Tough thorny bushes tore at our clothes. The sound of running water grew louder and a narrow track appeared. I stopped.

'Wonder what made this track?' Sam said as he peered ahead.

'Hope it wasn't that thing that roared in the night.' Ryan had made sure he stayed in the middle of the group.

'Scared are you Alvin?' Zach said – but from behind.

'Yeah,' I said. 'I'll let you go first.'

We went more slowly after that. Sam kept looking over his shoulder at the shadows. Then we were out of the trees, onto a river bank.

'What are those?' Zach stopped and pointed.

In front of us a huge flock of weird birds was spread out by the river. They looked like a cross between a chicken and a duck – ugly scrawny things with a smell worse than the school loo. There were hundreds of them, possibly thousands. The river bank had been trampled to bare earth.

The birds stayed almost silent, no squawking or birdsong, only the occasional rustling of their feathers. Even when we walked into the flock, the birds didn't appear very interested. Zach still had his branch in his hand. With a jump and a yell he smashed the branch down on the first small bird, killing it and breaking the branch. That got them moving. With a loud rushing sound they took to the air. Zach held up the dead bird as though expecting praise.

'Brilliant Zach. You've scared them off,' I said.

Zach looked at me and took a step forward. So did I. Zach's face reddened and his eyes narrowed. I didn't move and I saw Zach's shoulders slump. He was probably remembering my brother's leg-ripping threat.

'At least I've got some food, better than you've done.' Zach tried to reassert himself, but his voice quivered. 'Anyway, they've all come down again.' He pointed ahead, finding something to take the attention away from himself.

Zach was right. The birds had flown around in an arc and just landed further along the river bank. It didn't take much to catch them. They'd struggle when you'd caught them but Sam seemed to know what to do. I thought it was pretty gruesome but he picked up the birds and twisted their necks until they were dead. I let him get on with it. Zach was still smashing away with a new branch – more club-like, and I thought he was imagining smashing me.

'I think we've got enough.' I looked at the mangled pile of dead birds. 'Let's take them back to the cave.'

'What are they?' asked Zach's other follower, who had stayed very quiet. 'If they aren't chickens or ducks, then what are they?'

'Chuckerns?' Ryan suggested and that name stuck. 'Do you think we can eat them?'

'No idea,' I replied. 'I've no idea what we should do with them.'

Zach sneered at my answer, but he didn't have any ideas either.

'Pluck them and draw them,' Sam said quietly.

'Oh, so you're an expert eh?' Zach poked him with his stick. 'Like you ever know anything.'

'My dad was a butcher. He showed me what you do with chickens. You pull all their feathers off. Then you cut out their guts. 'Drawing' is the bit when you cut out the guts.' Sam sounded convincing.

'Great Sam,' I said. 'You're in charge of plucking and drawing.'

Zach sneered again.

I went down to the river, splashed water on my face and took a drink. I was trying to stay calm. Sam stuck close.

'How do we know if the water is safe to drink?' Sam said.

'We don't,' I snapped, getting fed up with stupid questions. But we needed Sam if these birds were going to be of any use so I tried to be friendlier. 'But I guess no one has died yet and we've all drunk it.'

We headed back. Coming out of the forest I looked up and saw smoke billowing from the cave and the others wiping their streaming eyes. I shouted something and that seemed to set them off screaming and running back under cover.

Then I understood. We were carrying a pile of dead birds, blood and feathers stuck to us. Sticky, thorny; bits of bush, tree and creeper had torn our clothes from the forest. Zach, bloodied from head to foot, hair matted with pieces of massacred bird, waved his killing club in the air.

In some other place this might have been a joke. But no one was laughing here. Zach made it worse by letting out a yell and making a mock charge, club swinging. When the rest calmed down they tried to make excuses for their panic.

'It was the smoke in our eyes,' Jack said. 'We didn't recognise you. You were all covered in stuff.'

'We thought we were going to be attacked by savages,' Stevie added.

We hadn't fooled Jenna who just pointed at the blood stained mass of feathers and said, 'We're not eating those.'

'What are they?' several voices asked.

'Chuckerns,' replied Ryan.

'Yuck,' said Stevie.

'It's them or nothing,' I said. 'Sam knows what to do.'

Everyone turned to Sam and he froze. Sam really didn't look like he knew anything. That was the person I remembered at school. Sam would make out he knew stuff, but it was made-up, fantasy. I'd believed him this time, thinking he wouldn't make up things about his dad who had just died. Another one of my great thoughts.

'You've no idea ... pathetic ... useless pile of ...' And Zach hurled one of the birds at Sam. It caught him in the face and he fell to the ground.

'I do know,' Sam said, looking up. 'Dad was a butcher, it's just ...'

'Just what?' Zach threw another bird. 'Just that he's as useless as you?'

'No he isn't ... wasn't.' Sam started to get up and I could see he was about to do something stupid and fly at Zach. Bad idea even if Zach wasn't holding a club. I was tired and hungry. Zach did have a point – Sam seemed to have no idea.

'Sam do you really know what to do?' Jenna stood in his way.

Sam stopped, turned to her and nodded.

'Well get on with it.'

Sam still looked confused and it was Matt who walked over to Sam and took Jenna's place in front of him, using his body to shield Sam from the taunts.

'What do you need to do first?' Matt asked in his slow voice.

'You need to c ... c ... c ... cut their heads off,' Sam stammered. 'But I haven't got a knife.'

'Could you use this?' Jack asked as he slid himself across the cave. He held a piece of stone which could have broken off during the earthquake. It looked like flint. 'I know it's very sharp because I sat on it,' Jack said.

Matt took the stone and showed it to Sam, who just shrugged. Matt knelt on the ground, picked up one of the birds and holding it with one hand hacked off the head with the sharp stone. It took him several attempts. Someone puked.

'Go for it, Matt,' Zach cheered, although he looked a little green.

The headless bird brought Sam back into action. 'Now you stick your finger in its neck and pull out stuff – I think it's called the crop.'

Matt gave the bird to Sam without saying more. I thought it was a waste of time. But Matt's help seemed to work. Sam took over and scooped something out with his finger.

'Now you've got to pull off the feathers – pluck them.' Sam gave a running commentary as he pulled at the feathers. I wondered if he was trying to sound like his dad. Sam found the feathers hard to pull out and it took a long time.

'Sam, this is going to take for ever – we'll have to help.' Jenna grabbed one of the birds. 'Matt can you cut some more heads off and we can all do this.'

'No way!' said Demelza, who had been unusually quiet. She tried to strike a pose, one hand on her hip, pouting. It looked stupid. No one took any notice of her, even her own two hangers-on.

'No plucking – no food,' Zach said with a nasty grin.

Demelza pouted again, this time at him. He looked confused and his blush was red enough to be seen even through the mess of chuckern still plastered on his face.

Demelza turned to her friends with a mischievous smile.

'Demelza's got him. As if we don't have enough problems,' Jenna whispered. At the time I didn't get what she meant.

In the end we all tackled the birds and, with a bit of help from Mary and Matt, everyone ended up with a scrawny headless chuckern with most of the feathers removed. It smelt, we smelt and the feathers stuck to us. There were a few birds left over.

'What now? Do we cook them?' Mary asked.

'Um ... not quite.' Sam, having finished plucking his bird, had been staring at it while we caught up. 'You've got to make a hole near its bum and pull out the guts.' He tried, and failed, to make it sound easy.

His words met a stunned silence. Zach might be the only one holding a club, but everyone looked pretty angry. Sam had to do it. He took the sharp flint piece from Matt and chopped into the bird's belly. The stone sliced into the soft skin, exposing a tangled mess of guts.

I watched him stick his fingers through the cut, into the bird, and with some wiggling he pulled out the squidgy innards, which he plopped onto the grass. They slithered on the slope, almost as though they were alive. Sam looked relieved, and rather proud. 'Just be careful when you do that, don't damage the guts, and get them all out,' he said, his voice sounding much firmer.

'Why?' asked Stevie, who had been crouching over Sam, watching everything he did.

'Dad always said you must remove all the guts ... something important about it. I can't remember exactly why, but he went on about it.'

'Because they stink?' Stevie suggested.

'Maybe.'

Sam poked the slithery mess with his sharp stone and the guts came apart. Stevie reeled at the smell.

Sam tackled a couple more birds before the rest of us tried to 'draw' our own chuckerns. It wasn't easy and I could see that not everyone carried out the task perfectly. Sam still didn't remember the really important thing his dad had told him. Soon all of us, smeared and bloody, sat near a pile of stinking innards.

'Next time we do this by the river,' Jenna said, looking at the mess of guts, feathers and birds' heads.

'Next time? How long are we going to be here?' wailed the ginger Sara.

Jenna leant over to me and said, 'That's the 'Other-Sara'. Sara and Other-Sara in case you get confused.'

'Remind me.'

'One Sara is blonde, the other is more ginger. The ginger one is Other-Sara.'

'Oh, right.' I was only half listening and I was confused. 'Any ideas on how to cook them?'

'Sara or the birds?' I wasn't sure Jenna was joking.

I looked at my chuckern. 'The fire's not much good.'

'We can't keep the fire burning in the cave if it's going to smoke like this.' Jack's leg made it difficult for him to get out of the smoke.

'Isn't the smoke meant to show the rescuers where we are?' the Sara who wasn't 'other' said.

'No one will find us without it,' added the other one, they were both looking at me. I wasn't answering.

'Not sure who or what might see the smoke,' Jenna replied for me. 'There isn't anything normal out there. Maybe we should only make the fire smoke if we hear something. But now it doesn't look any good for cooking.'

'It smokes because of all the green stuff on it. We need to use dead wood, as dry as possible.' Matt seemed to be a bit of a survival expert.

While we'd been searching for food, no one else had gone into the forest to get firewood. So they had just collected bits of bush from near to the cave – wet green bits of bush that burnt with a dense smoke.

'Let's go.' I set off to get some dry wood. After a few steps I turned. No one else had moved. 'Matt, Sam come on. And the rest of you.' I stood watching, feeling a bit stupid. Would anyone take any notice and follow me? They did, at least most of them came – slowly. Zach and Demelza held back with their group.

It was easy to find dead brushwood amongst the trees and soon we had a blazing fire near to the entrance of the cave.

'We should make a spit,' Matt said. 'You know, put the birds on a long stake and turn it over the fire.'

'Oh yeah?' Zach said sticking his bird onto the end of his club and holding it in the flames. The flesh soon burnt and the burning bird fell into the fire.

'Give me yours,' he said to Sam.

It went very quiet. Sam stared, looking frightened and confused. No one else moved. Did the others expect me to do something? I just wanted to work out how to cook my own bird and didn't see why this had to be any of my business. Sam looked as though he might refuse. Zach lifted his club slightly. Sam hung his head and handed his chuckern over.

'Good boy.' Zach knew how to make it so much worse.

A red-faced Sam shuffled off. Everyone watched him and no one helped. Sam started to prepare another chuckern.

The fire had burnt down a little, making it easier to get nearer to the hot ashes. Like Zach, each of us stuck a bird on the end of a stick and held it to the fire, trying not to set our chuckerns alight.

'How do you know when they're cooked?' Stevie had latched onto Matt.

'No idea. I guess you try one and see.' Matt pulled his bird out of the fire and took a bite.

We were all shouting, 'What's it like ...' 'Yeah, Matt, can we eat it? ...' 'Tell us ...' 'Hurry up! ... I'm starving.'

'Umm,' Matt replied with chuckern fat running down his chin. 'Tasty, well sort of tasty,' and he took another bite.

Matt's words set us all ripping the birds apart, eating every last piece of meat – cooked, partly cooked, or uncooked. Apart from munching, the cave remained quiet as we ate, except for Ryan who seemed unable to eat without farting.

I was sitting next to Jenna on a stone outside the cave. We watched the sun setting as the sky darkened and turned a deep orange before darkness settled. Only the moon and stars lit the sky. The smell of burnt chuckern still hung in the air. I'd told Jenna all about the teacher, well most of it, not the bit about seeing her at home.

'What do you think will happen?' I asked because I couldn't think of anything else to say.

'Why ask me?'

'No one else around, like you said before.'

'Maybe this is just your dream,' Jenna sounded rather hopeless. 'It sounded dream-like when you told me.'

'I suppose dream-like is better than you saying it was some drug ...'

'I said I was sorry.' Jenna made it clear that the subject was closed. You didn't win arguments with Jen.

'Ok it's a dream. You mean pinch me and I'll wake up?' I wasn't sure where this was heading.

Jenna was quick.

'Ow. That didn't work, we're still here.'

'Probably didn't pinch you hard enough.' I was lucky Jenna was smiling. Then she looked more serious: 'Have you worked out what that teacher meant by her promise?'

'No idea.' I picked up a stone, looked at the chipped flint absentmindedly feeling the sharp edge with my finger. 'I don't see how we're going to survive to find out anything, whatever she meant.'

'And I don't think we need to get the fire to smoke again – there's no one out there to see it.' Jenna got up and wandered off.

The fire still burnt with occasional flames making flickering shadows on the cave walls as each person tried to find somewhere to lie down, avoiding Zach who kicked anyone who came near him.

I stayed outside alone, staring out and trying to imagine what the teacher could have meant. Then when nothing made sense I ended up going over things from home. If they did chuck me out where was I going to go? Nothing seemed clear. Maybe being stuck here was the answer.

In the dark, grunts and howls started again in the trees. I gave up thinking and found somewhere to lie down, nearly treading on Zach – deliberately. I didn't expect to have a comfortable night and I was right, but the thing that Sam had forgotten made it so much worse.

It was a new noise that woke me up. Blonde Sara was the first. She had dealt with a chuckern by herself. Probably she hadn't understood what Sam had said and probably she had been too scared to ask for help. Sara groaned, ran to the cave entrance and threw up spectacularly – silhouetted in the light of the moon. A foul smell of half digested chuckern wafted into the cave. Sara wasn't alone for long. Soon there was a row of them – clutching stomachs, retching and moaning.

A little later I felt Sam tap me on the shoulder. 'I've just remembered what dad said.'

'What?' I shoved him away, holding my hands to my ears and trying to blot out the noise.

'He said you must get all the guts out whole and clean the inside otherwise bugs get into the meat.'

I had no idea what Sam was going on about.

'The bugs cause food poisoning – vomiting, diarrhoea; people can get very sick. It'll be worse because not everyone cooked them properly.'

I rolled my eyes although Sam probably missed that in the dark.

'Can't do anything about it now,' Sam sobbed.

'At least 'chuckern' was a good name,' I said wondering if I'd done enough to my bird.

Not everyone was sick. Sam and Matt had done a good job cleaning their birds and those they had helped were alright. I guess I was just lucky.

The first Sara slumped down, sitting with her back to the rock, holding her tummy, and it seemed with nothing left to bring up. Others joined her. Mary started taking water round to the sick, stumbling over rocks to fill plastic water bottles from the pool near the cave.

Other-Sara was the worst. She didn't stop retching, over and over again, her ginger hair matted and streaked. Jenna told me her friends had talked about the pills Other-Sara needed to take. Some strange disease that no one could pronounce. Mary tried to hold her hand, but let go when Other-Sara's body shook with another fit of retching. It went on for hours.

'What do we do with her?' Mary said to Jenna.

'How should I know?' Jenna shrugged her shoulders and sounded cross. That's more like Jenna, I thought, but it only lasted a second. Jenna changed her tone: 'I'll try her with some more water,' and she went and sat on the damp earth beside her.

The water made Other-Sara sick again.

Jack had taken on the task of keeping the fire going but stopped when he became exhausted, so the fire died down as the night drifted on. Only a faint red glow lit the cave, when I saw Other-Sara try to stand. She vomited one more time and groaned loudly before falling to the ground with a heavy thud. I heard the fall and yes, I knew something awful had happened, but like the others I went back to sleep in the silence that followed.

This time it was a poke that woke me. I opened my eyes, seeing Jenna's face about an inch away from mine, behind her the faint light of dawn.

'Wake up,' Jenna hissed in my ear.

'What?' I grunted.

'I think she's dead,' Jenna's voice cracked as she whispered the words.

'Who?' I muttered stupidly.

'Other-Sara, you idiot,' replied Jenna. 'I couldn't sleep and I've just checked on her. She's not moving.'

'What do you want me to do?' I tried to turn over. 'Too tired …'

Jenna hit me hard on the arm. 'We need to do something before the rest wake up. They'll go berserk.'

I shook myself awake. An irate Jenna was too difficult to resist and I followed her to where Other-Sara lay on the hard ground.

'How do you know she's dead?' I looked at her pale face shining in the early light. To me she looked more peaceful than when she'd been sick.

'I tried to wake her, but she doesn't move and she's icy cold. It was just like when I went to hospital with …' Jenna stopped, sounding too choked up to explain.

Matt appeared and a few others stirred, but no one else joined us.

'Should we do something?' Matt said in a hushed voice.

'What? Give her the kiss of life you mean?' I looked down

and shivered.

'Too late,' Jenna said. 'It's too late to do anything. She's dead, can't you see.' Jenna's whispers came in angry bursts. 'We need to move her. We need to ...' Jenna seemed to find it impossible to say what we needed to do, but in the shadowy light we carried the small body from the cave and down into the trees.

'What now?' asked Matt, looking at the lifeless form.

'I don't think there's anything we can use to bury her.' I looked around.

'Cover her up, I suppose,' Jenna said eventually.

In silence we covered her with earth and stones. It wasn't easy and took ages.

'Are we meant to say something?' The mound over her looked awful. I backed away from the grave. Neither Jenna nor Matt replied. In the end we all shuffled away saying nothing.

I knew that burials weren't a normal part of school trips, but I didn't think this was going to be the only one.

-4-

ANOTHER DAY

Leaving the grave, we stumbled back, not speaking, and sat on the rocks outside the cave. No one wanted to meet the others. Jenna hugged herself and shivered; silent tears streamed down Matt's face. I was staring into space, the sight of her body played over and over in my mind.

As the sky lightened the rest began to move. I wondered how we were going to tell them. I couldn't do it. I got up and left, scooping up a drink from the pool, I followed the cliff. I could almost feel Jenna's eyes burning into my back. I'd left them to explain and since Matt probably wouldn't know what to do, that meant I'd left Jenna to do it. I headed for the waterfall.

At the top of the slope I could see water crashing from the cliff and pounding the rocks below. The river ran out of sight towards the bank where we'd found the chuckerns. Thinking about the birds almost made me retch. Was there anything else to eat? Would we have to eat those birds again? The wide river foamed and frothed, plumes spouting into the air against the rocks; too dangerous to try and cross. Wherever we were, it seemed as though we were trapped. Were we all going to die like Other-Sara?

Not concentrating, I stumbled over a root. Looking up at the tree, it was loaded with purple fruit and I saw that many of the bushes were covered with red and black berries. Was any of this safe to eat? Other-Sara's pale face kept coming back to me; even though I was hungry I left the fruit and scrambled down to the river.

Early morning sunlight started to shine through the mist thrown up by the waterfall, but the mist made the air cold and I shivered. Along the rocky uneven river bank water swirled into pools. I tried to wash off some of the dirt and remains of chuckern. Then I heard movement in the bushes and I froze, listening. Nothing except the noise of the water. I started back.

'Sam make sure you always do my chuckerns properly.' Zach's nasty laugh met me as I neared the cave. Zach went on, 'And you can share them with me, just to make sure I don't get poisoned like that ...'

I stood at the entrance. Against the sun my body cast a large dark shadow across the cave floor. That seemed to stop him.

'Like what?' I said staring at Zach.

'Zach's been telling us how Other-Sara died – haven't you Zach? Tell us again,' Jenna said.

'Nooooooooooo.'

I heard wails from the back of the cave.

'Go on Zach. You do a great imitation of her retching noises.' Jenna twisted the knife.

Zach sneered and turned away.

I looked around the group. They were crying, tired, angry and frightened, surrounded by the remains of last night's awful meal. Zach had really wound them up.

I knew something was needed. 'We can't do anything about Other-Sara, but we've got to survive. If someone is going to break through that tunnel it could take ages, remember how much rock fell down behind us, we've got to keep going until ...'

'No one's going to break through that.' Ivy pointed to the back of the cave.

'Maybe, but I'd like to try and stay alive long enough to give them a chance.' I was almost shouting.

'How? How do we survive?' someone else called out.

'Look. I don't know what we should do ...' I searched for my words.

'That's true,' Zach said just loud enough for everyone to hear.

I wouldn't take much more of this no matter what Jenna said.

'Shut it Zach,' Jenna spat. The anger in her voice made Zach take a step backwards and he sat down next to his two followers.

'But we have to do something.' I poked the ground with my foot, this wasn't easy. I was doing what I'd said I wouldn't – making suggestions. 'Sam's told me why the chuckerns made us ill. And I don't like it but we've got to eat, so we'll have to eat chuckerns again.'

'No way,' Ivy cried out.

I had to go on now. 'Ivy we all feel like that. There may be something else. I've been over to the waterfall and there are trees with some sort of fruit. I guess you'll say they'll be poisonous.' I looked at her, she blushed and turned away. 'Anyway we should check them out somehow.' Now they were all listening. I saw Jenna nod; it made me feel more confident. 'Even so, we need to get more of the birds.'

'We should clean them out in the river,' Sam said. 'It'll be safer.' His voice faltered, everyone looked at him. 'I ... I ... I didn't know,' he pleaded and sunk lower on the ground.

'It's not Sam's fault,' Mary said, her face reddening. 'We all should have realised the danger. We were too tired and hungry.

You can't just blame Sam.'

I knew we all did.

'At least if we clean them by the river we won't have more disgusting bits lying around here.' Jenna pointed to the stinking remains which added to the smell from the small piles of puke.

I wanted to find a way to persuade Zach to go hunting chuckerns again. I wanted him out of the way. I was sure everyone else wanted the same to happen.

'We'll do some hunting again – eh, Zach? Nothing like smashing a few bird brains?' Ryan said and surprised them all.

'Too right,' replied Zach, jumping to his feet, club in hand. 'Come on Sam, cleaning to do!' and Zach led the four of them off.

'I'm coming too,' Demelza said with a small smile while Zach's eyes grew wider. 'And you two.' She waggled her finger at the only two who seemed to stick with her.

Zach tried more swaggering as I watched him lead the strange group down the hill. After a few steps Demelza looked back over her shoulder and gave me a small smirk. They disappeared into the trees. I turned to Jenna expecting trouble.

'I'll tell you about it,' she said. 'I watched you run off ...'

'I didn't run ...'

'Whatever you did, you left me to explain.'

'Sorry.'

'First you need to know who they are, the three left from our Junior school – now we've just one Sara. Then Stevie –.'

'Who wines, moans, and snivels?'

'You forgot sobbing, whimpering and other annoying stuff. Then your girl of the moment and she's called Emma.'

'My girl?'

'Yeah the one who keeps staring at you, like you're some superhero.'

'I thought she was called Lisa.'

'No. Idiot. Lisa's in our year although she did only join last term.'

'I've not been around much this year.' I looked down at the ground thinking about home.

'You can't miss Lisa because Matt follows her around and she keeps trying to get away.' Jenna pointed over to where Lisa was sitting and there was Matt shuffling towards her. 'But back to the younger lot – your hero-worshipping one is Emma.'

I'd mostly given up trying to work this out.

'After you'd run off, the three of them came out of the cave together and asked where Other-Sara had gone. I tried my best but I didn't know how to say words like 'dead' or 'buried' without sounding like it was some horror movie. They started howling, screaming, and running into the cave, shouting at the back wall as if the louder they shouted the more hope of rescue coming from the other side. I guess you kept away from that.'

'Didn't hear, I was ...'

'Oh yeah? Anyway that really set Zach off. He said things like at least you don't have to remember that stupid name – now there's only one of them – and that wound everyone up.'

'But not enough to do anything?' Since no one had ever bothered to do anything about Zach before I didn't think they'd start now.

'No. No one is up for that fight.' Jenna looked up. 'Maybe except you?'

'You keep stopping me.'

'It got worse because with most of us shell-shocked Zach

started going through everyone's packs in the hope of finding something to eat. Sara tried to stop him taking her pack but he just slapped her hard in the face.'

'Sorry,' I mumbled.

'What for? For wandering off?' she replied. 'What are you meant to do? I want to blame you, but what for? Why should it be up to you to tell them someone's died?'

'Why do you think Demelza wanted to go with Zach?' I couldn't think of anything better to say. 'Almost like she fancies him.'

'He certainly fancies her – his tongue was hanging out when she said she would go with him. I guess she'll use him to get what she wants. Demelza saw Sara getting slapped. She'd rather be the one doing the slapping than getting hit herself.'

'Probably she doesn't think we'll do anything,' I said.

'Now Zach's gone we need to do something with that lot.' Jenna pointed at the huddle at the back of the cave and with a brisk voice that sounded nothing like her usual self she called, 'Sara, Stevie, Emma – follow me.' She marched them out of the cave.

I watched her go and then looked at the others. Jack, still in pain, could only shuffle around the cave on his bottom.

'Sorry, but I think the only thing I can do is to keep the fire going.' He looked at the small heap of embers which he'd been trying to keep alight by poking them. 'But I can't collect any wood,' he said moving his leg slightly and flinching with pain to make his point.

'I can get wood,' replied Matt and started to set off towards the forest.

I held up my arm to stop him. 'Good idea, but first why don't you go with Ivy and … um … Lisa to look at the fruit on the trees. Then you could bring some wood back with you.'

Matt seemed to like the idea. I didn't want to tell them about the noise I'd heard by the river, but thought it a good idea if all three stayed together.

'And me?' Mary asked, hearing that I was handing out jobs. It was as though once I'd started doing it I couldn't stop.

'As far as I could see there's no way out of here on the waterfall side, I'm going to have a look the other way.'

Jenna's words about this being my dream were on my mind. There must be something I hadn't found yet. I didn't want to feel like this but was there a choice? It wasn't just Zach. If we had any chance then we needed to find a way out of here. There was no one else around to make any decisions. Mine might be wrong and useless but someone had to do it. If this place wasn't going to kill us off then Zach would probably do it on his own.

I looked at Mary, probably I should have checked this out with Jenna but I said, 'Do you want to come?'

'Ok,' Mary said sounding rather nervous.

'I won't eat you,' I grinned.

'I wouldn't be so sure.' Jack butted in from his place on the ground.

'Of course I'll go,' Mary said with greater confidence.

'No screaming,' I said in a firm tone.

Mary blushed. 'Sure, no screaming,' and she turned to Jack. 'You'll be alright?'

'No problem,' said Jack, a bit slow with his reply.

'Jenna will be around if you need help,' I suggested, but thinking perhaps it wasn't Jenna that Jack wanted.

Mary decided any exploring needed us to carry at least one backpack, with a couple of water bottles. Her pack had contained a waterproof jacket, which she took; mine had a pair of waterproof trousers several sizes too small. I left them behind.

'Come on,' I said in the end while muttering about 'fussing'.

Mary turned to Jack and gave him a wave. We set off. As we left I called out to Jenna. She was clustered with the younger ones. The look on her face made me think that I really should have checked this out with her before I wandered off. Mary seemed to be whistling. I thought she should stop.

-5-

THE NOTE

I wanted to have a look at other caves I thought I'd seen in the cliff. They happened to be in the opposite direction to everyone else, and particularly Zach.

The ground on the waterfall side of our cave may have been cleared by a rock fall, but the opposite direction was completely overgrown. Trying to stay next to the cliff meant we were soon fighting through tall bushes. It was slow but I wanted to make it easier to get back the same way. Mary's long hair caught in the thorns and she stopped to tie it back.

Pushing through the bushes I headed for the first cave and stopped, waiting for Mary to catch up.

'Do we want to go in?' Mary said peering at the long wet creepers hanging from the rock which half covered the entrance.

'I'll go,' I said ducking into the cave, disturbing a solitary chuckern which flew past my head towards Mary.

Mary jumped and gave a loud gasp, stifling a scream. I looked round with a half grin and she went red. I went into the cave but it only stretched a few yards into the cliff, damp and dark and empty.

'Nothing here.' I backed out.

Further along the cliff we found more caves and after the first one Mary went in with me. Every cave had the same musty smell and nothing other than a few more chuckerns. One was a bit larger.

'Big enough to move into if we had to get away,' said Mary.

'Away?' I didn't understand.

'Away from Zach.'

The way she said it made me feel that she was hoping I'd do something about Zach. I certainly didn't see why we should move out. If anyone was going to move it would have to be him. Although being so tired and hungry made me wonder if I could make that happen unless everyone backed me up. Would they?

We pushed on. The bushes became thicker and we couldn't keep next to the cliff. Anyway the cliff seemed to end a little further away. I thought we might as well turn back, but we could hear running water, so we pushed on. It seemed as though the way was a little easier. Had someone else been here before? I wasn't watching where I was going. Mary stopped and I crashed into her.

'Help!' Mary yelped.

We'd fallen together into bushes at the edge of a sheer drop. I'd only just heard Mary's cry above the roar of water below.

'Was that a scream?' I shouted and gave another small grin as I got up and pulled her up. She smiled and didn't answer. We moved back a little and I moved back a little further away from Mary.

'Is this the same river that makes the waterfall?' I said looking at the crashing water below us.

'I guess so. I think it must run past the chuckerns and then curve round and back to the cliff.'

'That means we are stuck here. Cut off by the river and the cliff. There's just the cave and the forest. I can't see what she meant about ...'

'What?' Mary looked puzzled.

I'd stopped as I realised Mary knew nothing about the words Miss Tregarthur had shouted at me. 'Nothing, something Jen said. Anyway there's no way across the river here either.'

'Trapped.' Mary gave a sob.

'Looks like it.' I threw a rotten branch into the foaming water and watched as it smashed against a rock before disappearing into a gorge carved in the steep black rock.

'Let's go back,' I said beckoning Mary and wondering what she would say to Jenna. Falling together had been a bit too complicated. I turned to the path we'd made.

Mary stopped again and I saw her looking around as though searching for something.

'Anything?' I called.

'No, but there's something wrong here.'

'Difficult to find one thing more wrong than everything else. Like what?' I asked.

'Dunno really, but something made me shiver. As though something awful has happened here.' Mary clasped her arms around herself.

I poked about in the bushes for a few moments. 'Nothing I can see. I guess we might as well go back to our cave.' We hadn't found anything but I felt Mary was right; there was something strange about this place. Strange but not helpful.

Suddenly Mary stopped once more. 'Wait! Look – is that another cave?' She pointed.

A shift in the sun had exposed the entrance – a large dark gap in the rock face.

'Come on.' I was sure this had to be something important.

We fought our way back to the cliff. I forced the way through, even thicker thorny bushes tearing at my skin. I was in a hurry. Battered and grazed, we finally stood outside a vast gash in the stone reaching high into the cliff. In front of us another cave stretched back into darkness.

'What's that smell?' asked Mary.

'Smells like Ryan,' I sniffed.

'Worse than that,' replied Mary.

'Impossible!' We both laughed, forgetting where we were for a moment. But the sound of our laughter echoed back from the depths of the cave and in silence we walked in.

As my eyes grew accustomed to the dark I could see several smaller caverns linking together at the entrance; a huge slice of stone hung over the opening to one of them.

'Like a guillotine blade,' said Mary touching the rock.

'I can see something.' I ducked under the stone. In the shadows there was a pile of bones.

'They look very old,' Mary said but she didn't follow me.

'Good thing.' I held up one massive bone, handing it to her as I came back out.

'It's like something from a museum,' Mary said looking at what seemed to be a large jaw bone which still held several sharp pointed teeth, and a broken, curved, tusk. Something crawled out of one of the tooth sockets and Mary threw the bone away with a small gasp.

There was nothing else in the other caverns but at the back of the cave a narrow entrance seemed to lead to a passage going into the cliff. I had to crawl to get in and it stretched round a bend into complete darkness. A tunnel had led us here – maybe another one would lead us out.

I called to Mary: 'Stay there, while I look a bit further.'

I soon came back to tell her: 'It goes on and on and it goes upwards. I can see a faint light, so it must go somewhere.'

'Do you think we should go and get the others?' Mary said slowly.

'Probably, but I'm going to see. It may be the only way out of here.' I turned back to the tunnel and said over my shoulder, 'You can go back if you like,' thinking it might be better if she did go back.

'I'm coming,' she said in a rather small voice.

After the first bend, the tunnel climbed steeply and a faint glint of light appeared in the distance. We had to crawl again at one point. As we went on the light grew stronger.

Again we heard the sound of water. Another bend and then the tunnel ended. We stumbled out into daylight.

'Look. Look!' Mary shouted while I just stared around me.

We stood on a short rock ledge. Below, the river churned and crashed amongst the rocks. On the other side the cliff towered above us. Its sides green with moss and long creepers. Several rock falls looked to have worn away the steep sides. It was an amazing sight but that wasn't what made Mary shout.

'Steps,' Mary shouted again, moving to get a better view.

There at the end of the ledge a few rough steps led upwards to an overgrown path zigzagging up the cliff sides. It looked steep, slippery with rain water, and unsafe.

'No one's been up there for years,' Mary said. The path was covered with creepers and plants.

'Someone must have made it once. Maybe it's the way out.'

'Come on then.' Mary made for the path.

'Eh?' Now I was surprised and stood back and let her pass. I followed behind.

Up and up we went, slipping and dislodging rocks on the steep slope. Higher and higher. After a while the path became a narrow ledge almost carved into the cliff side. Rounding one bend a large jagged rock had slipped, blocking the way.

Mary stopped. 'No way around this,' she said, turning to me.

'Let me try.' I brushed past.

Hanging on to the fallen rock I inched my feet along the ledge. Small stones fell and I had to kick them away. The stones tumbled into the air, seeming to fall forever before crashing on to the ground below. Stretching up I grabbed at a sharp edge and heaved myself towards the path. A crack echoed in the dark. A huge chunk of stone came away in my hand and I started to slide, frantically grabbing at any hold. The rock piece smacked my shoulder as it fell past, crashing all the way down and hitting the bottom with an echoing boom.

'Alvin!' Mary screamed.

I had scraped down the rock losing grip until my fingers clung to the ledge. My feet flailed in the air, scrabbling, as I fought to find a foothold.

'Alvin!' Mary screamed again.

Forcing against the burning pain in my shoulder I moved one hand further along the ledge, then the other, inch by inch. More stones fell. I looked down, that was a mistake and my head swam, my arms weakened. Too far to get to the safety of the path in front and no way back. I grabbed for one of the slimy creepers. It felt too thin to hold. I pulled and it broke. I grabbed for another, it felt stronger. It was my last chance. I held on, let go of the edge and kicked away, trying to swing sideways, grabbing for the ledge. My fingers missed, my shoulder smashed into the cliff, the pain shot through my whole body and I bounced back out over the void.

Mary let out her third scream.

Now I was swinging faster towards the rock face. My shoulder about to hit again, no chance I could hold on again if that happened. I heaved on the creeper and threw myself upwards; nothing left if this didn't work. My fingers clasped the edge. It was not enough. My strength was failing as a terrible weakness crept up my arms, my fingers started to slip.

'Save him! Keep my promise!'

The strange words seemed to come from behind me. The words burnt into me, turning my weakness into fury.

'I'm saving myself,' I yelled at the rock. 'Myself.' And I hauled, screaming 'Myself!' with each pull before I lay on the path, panting hard and fast.

'Alvin?' came Mary's quieter voice.

'I thought ... you ... promised ... not ... to scream,' I panted the words out.

'Sorry, but didn't you scream too?'

I heard Mary's half laugh, half sob. I lay still but what next? Should I persuade Mary to go back or could I get her around the rock?

'I'm not going back,' Mary said before I had time to think.

Her voice came from above me. Holding several of the creepers, she had climbed up to the top of the rock blocking the path. Lighter than me, she grabbed another bunch and abseiled down to join me.

'You alright?'

'That looked easier,' I muttered. 'Wish I'd thought of that.'

'You didn't ask me,' Mary smiled.

'You still screamed,' I said rubbing my shoulder.

'Let me look,' Mary said as she crouched over me and pulled back the remains of my blood-soaked shirt. 'Looks mostly grazed. Can you move it?'

I winced as she lifted my arm. 'Seems to work. Any other advice Nurse Mary.'

'I hate that name.'

'Don't you want to be a nurse then?'

'I did once and because I kept saying it I suppose I haven't much choice now.'

'Certainly no choice if we don't get out of here.' I struggled to my feet and took a swig from the water bottle that Mary offered me. 'Let's go on.' I plodded off along the path. We still had a lot further to climb but no more rocks barred our way.

Eventually we neared the top and as the path became less steep I speeded up, then ran, we both ran, almost leaping over the top of the rim, and stood, squinting, in the sunlight.

'There's nothing here,' Mary said as she collapsed on to the grass.

I sat with my head in my hands, staring at the path that snaked into the gloom far below. There was no sign of rescue here, no sign of anything at all and, worse, I knew we would have to make the trip back down the path. That rock again. I didn't think Mary's route was an option on the way back.

'Can't see why anyone made the path.' I looked up.

'How's the shoulder?'

'Just a graze, fine, no problem.'

'Let's look around a bit anyway.' Mary poked me into action and we got to our feet.

'It looks like ... er ... the top of a cake.' I tried to describe the shape of the landscape, but with food on my mind. The grass covered land sloped gently away from us and up to the top.

'More like a muffin,' suggested Mary, looking at the cracks
and ridges. 'A stone muffin.'

'Whatever it is we can't eat it.' My stomach rumbled.

It didn't take long for us to discover we were standing on
a massive solitary mound, bigger than a hill. Almost circular,
with vertical cliffs falling from the domed top where we stood.
It really was a bit like a muffin. We wandered around the edge.

'Can't eat it but we could fall off quite easily.' Mary stepped
back.

We walked on carefully. Below us the land was a mixture of
forests and grassland. Nothing to suggest there were people
anywhere.

'Can't see any other way down,' I said peering over the side.

'What are those?' Mary gasped and pointed a finger at something moving in the trees below.

'Elephants?' I saw the shapes at the bottom of the cliff, they
looked large even from where we stood.

'Not with curved tusks like that,' said Mary.

'Mammoths!' we shouted together.

'Then this is some sort of Lost World.' I remembered Sam's
words.

We stared at the huge woolly shapes.

'It's just not possible,' Mary whispered.

The lumbering beasts moved further into the trees, out of
sight, leaving a trampled empty space.

'Earthquakes, death and disaster, mammoths – what next?'
Mary said as we moved further round the cliff edge. A little
later I was looking down and pointed. 'I think that's Matt. We
must be above our cave.'

From this height we could see how the river curved from the waterfall, marking out a tongue of land. We were stuck. Water on one side and the cliff face of the muffin-mound on the other. Over the river the trees soon gave out to a wide green empty plain but I couldn't see any way to get across.

'That means we're probably safe from other animals as long as nothing can swim the river,' Mary said, looking at me as though she hoped I would agree.

'Safe and trapped,' I replied, but I still thought there were a lot of trees on our side and we didn't know what might live amongst them. Some of the scuttling sounds we heard at night might mean larger animals were nearby. And I had heard that noise down by the river, what made that?

'At least the mammoths are on the other side.'

'Good, unless we wanted to eat one.'

Mary looked at me as though I had gone crazy.

Wandering around the hill and watching the mammoths had taken time. The sun started to go down in the sky making it cooler. A little further ahead we saw two huge black stones, much larger than anything else, with one stone balanced on top of the other. We were going towards them without any real sense of purpose.

'I suppose we'd better go back down,' I said looking at the sky.

Mary stopped, staring at the stone shapes. 'They remind me of something.'

'What?'

'When Miss Tregarthur was going on about the moor she kept pointing to the top of the hill where she was heading. She called it 'Hanging Stone Hill'; there were two stones balanced one on top of the other. She had planned to take us to them on the walk. She seemed quite frantic to make sure we got there.'

'Did you hear her call out when we went into the tunnel?' I'd only shared this with Jenna.

'No, I was too scared. What did she say?' Mary was looking at the stones and didn't really seem to be listening. I stopped and wondered if I should tell her.

'Go on,' Mary said turning back.

'Dunno really. I might have imagined it. Perhaps she said something completely different. Jumbled her words in the wind.' I knew I sounded embarrassed.

'Just tell me,' Mary said loudly.

'I thought she said something about keeping her promise and about saving someone.'

'Saving who? One of us?'

'Yeah probably. Maybe she meant Jack. Maybe she knew he'd lag behind.'

'That's rubbish. She couldn't have known that. And you're sure she said something about keeping her promise?'

'No, I'm not sure,' I said with a harder note in my voice. She was grilling me and I didn't like it. 'I'm not sure of anything. Have you got any ideas?' I wasn't going to tell her that I thought I'd heard the same words on the climb just now.

'Yes. Let's check out the stones.' She pointed at the rocks up ahead. 'These stones are much bigger but they're the same sort of shape as the ones on the hill we were going to. Miss Tregarthur said they were important and that people left messages for each other under them ... in old times. Maybe she left some clue for us.' Mary ran to the stones. 'There must be something.' She started searching.

I joined her, but there was nothing to find. 'Useless. Let's go.'

I was worried about the fading light.

'Please, let me look under here, help me move this boulder.' Mary tugged at a large stone which must have broken off from one of the rocks.

'Ok ...' I didn't think there was any point but Mary obviously thought it important.

'There is something.' Mary scrabbled in the dirt and pulled out a small rusty tin. Sitting on the grass with the tin between us, Mary bent and prized it open with her fingers. Inside we saw the decayed remains of a thin, hand written, notebook. As the light shone onto the yellowed pages they started to disintegrate. She had only a few seconds to read aloud the words written on the inside of the back cover:

> Dad is really sick. I think he's going to die. I'll have to go back on my own. I have to finish this. I promised him. Then I have to save David. I promised.

We saw the name 'Alice' at the bottom of the page before the paper fell apart and revealed no more secrets. The tin turned to dust in her hands.

'We know who Alice was,' Mary said with a stony voice.

'Who?'

'Alice Tregarthur. That's her name. She's been here before. You didn't imagine the words about her promise – or saving someone.'

'It still doesn't tell us anything useful.' I looked at the pile of dust. It was already blowing away in the breeze.

'She must have been leading us here. She must have had a reason. This promise. Then her dad. It's just more confusing. And where is she now?' Mary looked around her.

'I saw her get hit during the earthquake. Pinned down by a boulder. I guess we should have gone back and helped her. I should have gone back and helped her.'

Mary gave me a weird look. 'Alvin going back to help someone?'

'Yeah, well, maybe if I had we wouldn't be in this mess.'

'If you'd gone back we'd never have got out of that earthquake. We'd all have died.'

I was embarrassed again by her words so I said, 'Probably we'll still all die.'

Mary said quickly, 'If Miss Tregarthur was here, then she did get back somehow. We've just got to find out how.'

'Not sure we'll ever know,' I yawned. I was tired, hungry and defeated. 'I'm not sure we can make it down now. It's getting dark. I don't suppose you have anything to eat in your pack?' I gave her backpack a hopeful look.

'Sorry, just water.'

'I wish you hadn't mentioned muffins.'

'Perhaps there's something else under the stone.' Mary started scrabbling again in the soil near to where she had found the rusty tin. I stretched out on the grass. We couldn't make it down the path in the dark; we'd have to wait for morning. I dozed off thinking that would take some explaining to Jenna.

A little later Mary shook me, hitting me with her next find:

'It's food,' she said and brushed off the dirt from a large rusty can. As she brushed, the remains of the label became faintly visible. She peered at it and gave a miserable groan.

'What?' I lunged for the tin.

'Dog food.' She handed it over. 'It's dog food – that teacher must have been crazy, why did she bring dog food?'

'Can you eat dog food?' I didn't care how crazy she might have been if we could eat whatever was in the tin.

'Doubt it. No idea. Anyway it's probably gone off.'

'Well I'm going to try.' I hammered at it with a piece of rock until the lid gave in. The thick brown gravy didn't smell too bad. I stuck my fingers into the gloopy mess and dragged out some lumps and stuck them in my mouth.

'Better than chuckern,' I mumbled with my mouth full. 'Want some?' I held the tin for Mary.

She looked doubtful, but as she watched me dip my fingers in for more she couldn't resist. We cleaned out the tin and then watched the sun as it started to fall behind the mountain peaks in the distance – exhausted, but at least a little less hungry.

'What now?' Mary pulled on her jacket as the breeze strengthened and clouds gathered.

'I suppose we should go back to the path. At least we might get a bit of shelter if we go down a little way.' I didn't like the look of the sky.

'I think we'll have to – and fast.' Mary jumped up, watching the clouds.

The weather changed with an eerie suddenness, from the earlier summery breeze to a gale. We ran towards the path, scared of being caught in the wind when we were so high up. Within seconds the rain began, lashing us as we slithered over the rim onto the path.

'We need to go further down,' I shouted, wanting to escape the weather.

In near darkness, we fingered our way along, keeping close to the rock wall, peering at the drop on the other side of the path. The wind blew a weird loud howl like someone blowing over the neck of a bottle. Then we came to the jagged rock.

'I don't know if we can get around or over this, even in the light,' I shouted again. I couldn't hear Mary's reply.

Crouching down we tried to get some shelter under Mary's waterproof jacket. Despite the wind and the rain we drifted into brief periods of sleep, too tired to resist.

In the deep night, a trickle of small pebbles and sand fell on the back of my neck. Sleepily I brushed them away. Then a larger stone struck my injured shoulder.

'Run!' I shook Mary awake and dragged her to her feet.

A shower of stones fell past us and the ground shook as we ran back up the path with no time to feel for the safety of the rock wall, terrified of being shaken into the void by another earthquake. We reached the rim, but the gale hammered rain down on us, forcing us back to crouch on a ledge.

'Hold on!' I screamed, trying to make my voice heard above the wind as I wrapped my arms around a rock.

Mary was holding – mostly on to me. And we waited. Each time we thought about moving, another tremor rocked the ground.

'What do we do?' Mary said after a while.

'No idea. Wait. Wait and hope.'

'Do you think we'll ever get out of here?'

We couldn't sleep and I thought Mary was just saying things that came into her head. I didn't reply.

We spent more minutes not speaking until Mary started again. 'Jenna said you've got trouble at home?'

'I've always got trouble at home.' I wasn't sure I wanted to talk about this.

'Jenna said this time it's much worse.'

'She's right there.' Another tremor hit us and I held on more tightly while we waited for it to stop.

'Well?' Mary tried again.

'You want me to tell you all about it?' I snapped.

'Might as well. Pass the time.'

'Oh, so my life story is only worth hearing to stop you being bored?'

Now it was Mary's turn not to answer.

But she'd started me off, taking my mind away from this place, taking me back to the mess that I'd left. In the end I just blurted it out: 'Dad's in jail – again – along with my brother. Mum's gone off with some bloke. They left me with my aunt. She's had enough of me and says I've got to get out when I'm 16. That enough for you?'

'Sorry,' Mary said slowly and that was the end of any conversation. But it didn't end my thoughts about home and Mum and Dad. Mum had been the only one I felt was on my side. Then she just vanished, left me with no one. How could she do that?

Finally as the thin light of dawn appeared the tremors stopped and the weather calmed. I let go of the rock and climbed back out onto the wet grass; Mary followed.

'It's over,' I said not knowing whether that was true.

We finished the rest of the water.

'That tremor might have re-opened the tunnel back to the moor,' Mary wondered aloud.

'We need to get down and see.' I yawned and looked at the path.

'What about the rock in the way?'

'No point in worrying about it now. We'll find out when we get to it.' I was too tired to deal with more questions.

We set off, making slow progress in the half-light.

'It's gone,' said Mary after we had been walking, sliding and slipping down the path. 'The rock's gone. The tremor must have moved it.'

Stones and grassy lumps littered the way, but no rock blocked the track. We found it at the bottom.

'Wouldn't like to have been under that when it fell.' Mary stared at the jagged mass.

'Come on.' I made for the passage. If the tremor had destroyed the tunnel then we were completely stuck. But only a few stones had fallen from the tunnel roof, which bruised us as we crawled in the pitch black, too early for any sunlight to show us the way.

'Look.' Mary pointed as we came out into the cave at the end.

The huge stone slice had fallen and closed off the cavern with the bones. I'd crawled under the stone on the previous day.

'You could have –' she started to say.

'Been crushed?' I finished her words before saying, 'Might be a better end than food poisoning,' and we walked on.

Exhausted and weary, bruised and battered, we headed for the cave. It had been very early when we started down the zigzag track and when we arrived back only Jack, still trying to keep the fire burning, saw us return. I motioned to him to keep quiet, as I made my way past the other sleepers and slumped down behind a rock. As I went to sleep I heard Mary holding a whispered conversation with Jack.

-6-

CONFRONTATION

I didn't get much rest and it wasn't only because I'd forgotten to check behind the rock before I lay down.

'Get me some water.' Demelza's impatient voice soon woke me.

She was pointing at Emma. I could see that Zach's lot had taken up the space near the cave entrance. Sandier ground, more comfortable and less smelly than amongst the rocks at the back. When I'd returned they slept on, not noticing me. Most of the rest, including Jenna, were deeper in the cave.

Later, Jenna told me that I'd somehow done something to help Emma back at school, something about getting her lunch box back from Zach. I didn't remember and to me it seemed unlikely. But perhaps Emma's lunch box experience at school made her believe that I would help her and she didn't move. Demelza repeated her order. Getting no reaction, she dug her elbow into Zach who leapt up holding his club.

'You heard – get the water,' Zach shouted. 'Or else ...' he added smacking the club against his open hand.

Emma stayed still. Now I slowly got to my feet. It must have been the way I did it because Zach looked confused. I enjoyed that, so I moved a pace forward.

'What's it to you, Alvin?' Zach said with a slight tremor in his voice.

I didn't answer. I just ran my fingers through my dark hair. This felt like a movie showdown. But what was this to me? Zach was a bully, but so what? Was it my business to do anything about it? Zach annoyed me, and his question annoyed me, but still I hesitated. Then I saw Jenna, and saw the wound on her head.

'What happened?' I asked, ignoring Zach.

'Him!' Jenna pointed at Zach who stood still wielding his club.

Last time Jenna had stopped me. Did she want to stop me now? It didn't look like it. Anyway Zach attacking Jenna made it personal. No matter what happened I wasn't going to let him get away with that. I also thought it might get me out of the interrogation I expected about being away with Mary for the night. Ok, we weren't some sort of item, but well ... I took another step forward, into the growing light.

'How about you getting me some water Zach?' I said in a slow firm voice. I was milking this challenge, my words echoed in the quietness of the cave. Zach swayed, looking bewildered and angry.

'She can do that.' He pointed his club at Emma.

'No. You get it Zach.'

'No way.' Zach turned to Ryan and the others, gave a half laugh as though it was a ridiculous suggestion and tightened his grip on the club, then he turned back.

I moved again – closer. I had to believe that he would lose his nerve. I had to expect that he was a true bully. I'd know that if he turned again to the others. That would mean he was scared to face me alone. I needed to see that move. Otherwise I didn't know what would happen. Maybe I'd run for it. I saw Zach's face tense. I saw him move his club back, ready for a strike.

I gave him a slight grin. 'Ready for this are you? Because I

74

say you're just a pathetic coward really.'

Zach tried a snarl, it looked weak. He looked at his club. Then he did it, turned to Ryan and nodded, expecting help. Too late, with his face turned the other way he didn't see the blow. I aimed for his soft belly with all my force, with the anger of everything that had happened to me. Perhaps it was unfair to take it out on Zach, but he got all that had built up, as though he was responsible for me getting thrown out of my home, for us being here, for Jenna. As Zach doubled with the pain of my fist I thumped him on the head and he went down, dropping his club. I looked over at Ryan. He looked away. I picked up the club and stood over Zach. My pulse was still racing and my breath coming hard, but it was over. Then the rest started up:'Hit him ...' 'Smash his face in ...' 'Kill him ...' came the shouts from hidden faces at the back of the cave.

Demelza, her friends and Zach's two followers tried to shuffle away; perhaps they decided they would be next. I tried to catch Jenna's eyes, but she avoided my look.

Zach had rolled himself into a ball, cringing and covering his head with his hands. He was a pathetic bully. But Zach wasn't going to do anything other than snivel from his position on the ground. Yes, he would try and get revenge later, but so what? And I wasn't happy with the shouted voices, hiding in the shadows.

'So, who wants to do it,' I said, offering the club for someone else to take, as I looked around the cave. No one moved. Jenna lifted her eyes and seemed to smile.

I hurled the club towards the forest, picked up one of the empty water bottles and held it towards Zach saying, 'Just get the water.'

Zach peeked out from behind his hands, not certain, expecting this was a trick.

I poked him with the bottle. 'Do it!'

Zach took the bottle, hauled himself up and limped out of the cave. His two followers did what they did best – followed. Demelza and the girls stayed still.

As soon as Zach left, the cave came alive with chattering voices. Ivy grumbled while Matt and Lisa argued about something. Jack poked the fire.

I squatted down next to Jenna. 'You Ok?'

'No, but I'll get over it.'

'What happened?'

'You wandered off with your little nurse for the night.'

Ok so I wasn't going to get away without the grilling. Even though Jenna was smiling a bit.

'Nothing happened,' I said looking back at Mary who gave more of a smile than I would have liked.

'Is that what she thinks?'

I didn't answer, a bit because I didn't know. Mary had hung on awfully tight during the night. I think Jenna read my thoughts.

'Whatever,' she said. 'Anyway you wanted to know what happened here.'

I nodded.

'After you left me with the kids –'

'You got them together. I saw you ...' Jenna's face told me I should shut up.

'So we got on with things. I thought they'd need to be busy after Other-Sara's death. That's what would happen at home, stop them asking questions, take their minds off it. That's what adults do. But it was the opposite, they dealt with it in their own way. Emma pretty much demanded to be taken to the grave and they set about tidying it up, making a marker with her name, and decorating it with flowers.'

'I guess we hadn't made a very good job of it.' Thinking of the grave made me shiver.

'That's what Sara said. But after that we did a bit of clearing in here. If we hadn't then where you lay down would have really smelt. That rock was the one most used in the night for the loo. We didn't do that well – you might want to wash a bit sometime.'

'Thanks,' I said giving myself an all over sniff.

'Things were going Ok. Ivy and the others found some fruit which seemed safe to eat, better than safe, it was delicious.'

'How did Ivy know it was safe?'

'I think we have to watch Ivy. I think she just ate it and didn't really care if it killed her. She's not just ordinary miserable. I'd guess she has full on depression, my mum had that.'

'Not much we can do about it.'

'Maybe not, but we don't want more deaths here.'

I thought more deaths were very likely but kept that thought to myself.

'Then Zach came back.' Jenna stopped and her shoulders dropped. Misery creeping over her face. 'They'd made Sam carry all the chuckerns, but he had bruises as well so I guess Zach had smacked him around with his club just for fun.'

It made more sense of everyone's shouts to hit him again and I felt that perhaps I hadn't punished Zach enough.

'Demelza was being really nasty, Zach put her up to it. I said something and Zach hit me. Knocked me down.' Jenna rubbed her head.

'Did you want me to hurt him more?'

'It was enough,' she smiled again. 'I stopped you before, so I can't complain now.'

At least she was smiling. But that stopped when she went on. 'They cooked the chuckerns but wouldn't let us have any. Just threw us the bones and scraps when they'd finished. Zach had Emma running to get water for him and the rest of his group. Jack got kicked for trying to stop them, his leg's bleeding again.'

I wasn't sure I wanted to hear any more. Jenna seemed to read that in my face.

'That's it really. They talked about tying us up. But I think they were just too lazy for that. It might have happened later if you hadn't come back.'

'Would it have made a difference if I hadn't stopped before?'

'Might have been worse, if you'd knocked him about then, he would have wanted revenge.'

'Not if I'd fixed him permanently.'

'Save it,' she said. 'Just don't leave us here alone again with him, unless you do fix him first.'

'Fine,' I said, with a casual shrug. I rather liked my role as an enforcer. But I looked over and caught Demelza's eyes. The hatred on her face told me this wasn't over. There were six of them. I wasn't sure I could count on any of the rest being any use if it came to all out war. Didn't we have enough problems?

Now Mary wanted to tell them about our exploration, but I said we should wait for Zach and the other two to return. None of them had come back or brought any water.

'Go and get them,' Jenna spat the words at Demelza and the two stared at each other.

Demelza didn't move. But Zach had been within earshot and he tried to swagger back into the cave, chucking the half filled bottle towards me.

'Tell them Mary,' I said handing the water bottle to Emma, which made Zach snort and Emma blush.

They listened in silence as Mary told them of our climb, the note and the mammoths. 'We wondered if the tremor might have opened the tunnel here,' she ended and looked at Jenna.

'We didn't feel anything,' Jenna replied sounding huffy. 'Very peaceful night we had here. It must have been really awful out on that mountain alone.' And she made the word 'alone' sound like a challenge.

Mary didn't react and I wasn't sure what she was thinking. But everyone started asking her questions about the note and the promise and everything else, in particular about the mammoths.

'Mammoths haven't been around for thousands of years,' Ivy mumbled from the back of the cave.

'So we are back in time,' Jack said.

'Might be, I suppose ...' Mary's voice trailed off.

'No, we are,' Jack raised his voice. 'It's the stones.' Jack paused and looked around, everyone was listening but no one seemed to grasp what he was saying. 'Mary said the stones you saw looked like the ones we were heading for on the moor only much bigger. Well, they are the same but thousands of years from now. After thousands of years they get worn down.'

'That makes sense.' Mary seemed to want to agree with Jack. Maybe I didn't need to worry about her. 'That fits with the mammoths. Something happened to us in the tunnel.'

'And Miss Tregarthur has been here before, but she's not here now.' I kicked at the fire. 'So we've no idea what she was doing or anything about this stupid promise.'

My words met silence until Stevie asked, 'What else lived at the same time as mammoths?'

'Can't remember,' said Jack.

'Might there be dinosaurs?' Stevie said in a hushed voice.

'We saw some very large bones in the cave by the river.' Mary had avoided giving too much detail about the jaw bone and the teeth.

'But that teacher – what's that about?' Ryan got a hard stare from Zach, who maybe thought he should be united in silence with him, but Ryan went on, 'There's just got to be something or someone here that she wanted to get back for.'

'We'll never find out, ever,' Ivy added.

'Rubbish Ivy. We will find out but only if we survive long enough. That means we have to do more stuff.' Jenna started to take over. Her injury didn't seem too bad. 'Ivy, can you and Lisa get some more fruit? Matt – more wood.' She hesitated as she looked at Zach, but again Ryan suggested that they went hunting. Zach seemed happy to have a reason to get out of the cave.

I thought Demelza would stay now Zach had been humiliated. I hoped that would happen. Then at least their group would be spilt. But the three girls trotted after Zach.

'How's the leg?' Mary knelt down next to Jack, by the fire.

'Worse.'

'Can I change the bandage?' Mary spent the morning looking after him. Making it very clear to Jenna that she needed to do it. Jenna seemed to look happy about it, but Mary gave me a sidelong smile when no one was looking which worried me.

'We need a proper toilet,' Sara suggested. 'No one took any notice when I said that before, but we've got to make one.'

'How?' asked Emma.

'Dig a hole,' Stevie replied.

Sara was right. Cleaning out the cave was too awful. It was getting pretty bad outside the cave as well. During the day everyone wandered off to find somewhere to use as a loo, and it was getting smelly and squidgy behind every rock and bush.

'How do we dig a hole?' Jenna said almost as though she was cross that the toilet wasn't her idea. 'Nothing to dig with.'

'Couldn't we use a hole that's already there? I found one earlier.' Stevie pointed to it.

'Have to make sure you don't fall in,' said Sam.

'Especially if it's full of ...'

'Shut up,' Emma interrupted Stevie. 'We just need to screen it off with some branches and it'll be fine.'

They fetched branches and tied them together with creepers and covered the branches with leaves and piled lumps of grass on top to stop the leaves being blown away.

Sam stood back and looked at it. 'Looks almost good enough to live in.'

'Won't be soon.' Stevie wrinkled his nose.

'It needs one more thing.' Jenna handed one of the flat stones to Sara, on it she had written 'WC' with a burnt stick. Sara lent the sign against the hut.

'Where's the loo paper?' I asked while helping Matt to stack the wood he'd fetched.

Lisa and Ivy had brought back more fruit. Jenna picked up one of the soft berries and threw it at me, catching me on the nose, we both laughed.

Ivy and Lisa had been swimming in one of the pools down by the river edge. They said they would show the others the best place to get in. It felt as though Jenna giving out instructions had made us all feel better.

Soon Zach came back bringing more chuckerns and bad feelings with him. But we ate, drank, and used the toilet. We did the same the next day, and the next. No clues to show what Miss Tregarthur had been doing. Ivy started scratching a mark for each day on the cave wall. The toilet stank. Zach brooded.

A VISITOR

I counted the scratches on the wall: Six scratches, six more days. No rescuers, no people, nothing. I didn't need to count the scratches. It was just something to do.

Jenna had started a sort of rota with cave cleaning, and wood collecting. No one could get Demelza to do anything. Zach would only hunt chuckerns.

Jack's leg had improved. He and Mary were spending more time together. She helped him hobble around and together they were doing things. One day, after Mary had helped him down to the river, they came back with a pile of mud from the bank. We all laughed at them but they took no notice. We watched as they moulded the mud into shapes and put them into the hot ash from the fire. The first efforts didn't work but it wasn't long before they'd made a real bowl.

'How did you know how to do that?' I asked looking at the round brown object.

'Read about it somewhere,' Jack replied as though making pottery in a cave was quite a natural thing to do.

'It's fantastic,' Stevie said, and he wanted to try making pottery as well.

But that was the moment Zach came back from a chuckern hunt as he liked to call it. Shadows from the six of them fell across the mouth of the cave. This looked like trouble.

'What's fantastic?' Zach's sneering voice sounded a challenge.

'Nothing,' Mary and Jack replied together.

'I know you're nothing,' Zach said with sniggers from behind him – loudest from Demelza. 'But what's that you've got there?' Zach pointed.

'A bowl,' said Jack after a pause.

'No it's not,' said Zach, crushing the fragile object under his foot.

Jack struggled to get up, but Zach kicked him and he fell to the ground with a shout of pain.

'I wouldn't get up again,' Zach taunted. Demelza gave a little giggle.

The numbers didn't look good. Matt and Ivy stood up but the rest just looked scared. Jenna might be fierce by nature but she wasn't built for fighting. Still I couldn't let this rest. I could see that they had a plan, so I needed to make that go wrong. I leapt up, grabbed Zach by the neck and held him next to the fire, facing the rest of them.

'So you've been planning have you? Coming up with some stupid little scheme.' I could see I was right by Demelza's snarl. 'Well you can tell us all about it. And if I don't like it then Zach goes in the fire with your chuckerns.' I felt Zach squirm so I tightened my neck hold and moved him closer to the flames. He must have felt the heat and his over dramatic scream made Demelza start talking.

'You can't fight us all.' She took a step forward, brave with the other four alongside.

I pushed forward as well. The remains of Zach's trousers started to burn. He screamed again and told Demelza to stop.

'Seems I can.' I was worried how long I could keep this up. I really might have to put him right into the fire unless we sorted this out. 'So tell me before it's too late.'

'Let him go first.'

I wasn't going to trust her. I could see that they were just waiting to jump me.

'Ok,' I said which surprised Demelza but she couldn't keep the slimy grin off her face. Then I turned Zach round and smashed his head into the side of the cave. It worked better than I'd hoped. Zach slid unconscious to the floor, or actually half into the fire. I stood back and let them pull him out.

'You've killed him,' Demelza hissed at me.

I was a bit worried that I had killed him but Zach soon let out a groan although he certainly wasn't up to anything else. Demelza made Ryan pick Zach up and carry him out of the cave.

'We're moving to another cave.' Demelza tried to make that sound like a victory. It didn't but they started to leave.

I turned to Jenna and gave a puzzled shrug. Was that their plan? Then Demelza threw her parting shot.

'Don't think you're going to get any more chuckerns. They're ours now. If you try then we'll throw you in the river.'

I didn't believe what Demelza meant until the next day. Sam had slipped off with Ivy. I guess they thought they should try and outsmart Zach's lot and get some more chuckerns. It didn't work out. Zach was waiting for them. They had to run for it.

Zach had found a cave further down the slope, nearer to the forest, and our track to the chuckerns went right past it. We could have made another route but they'd hear us. I didn't think we'd do well against them in the open. Zach wasn't going to let me take advantage of him again.

'We need to go down and have it out with them,' Jenna said to me outside the cave.

Bad idea. We could hear their shouts and laughter. I thought Zach was doing that on purpose. I wondered if we should retaliate and stop them coming up and getting fruit, but if they came in a group that would be difficult.

Then Zach appeared with the other two boys. I thought it looked stupid but they'd plastered themselves with chuckern blood and feathers as though they were warriors. Zach let out some sort of hoot before he stepped nearer.

'Tomorrow we want Emma. She's got to come down to our cave and work for us.'

'In your dreams,' Jenna called back.

'Else we're going to come up and burn you all alive in the night.'

Jenna and I had been alone, but everyone else heard Zach's threat. I heard gasps from inside our cave. Zach turned and left. The rest of our lot came out.

'What are we going to do?' Sam was trying to make himself stand tall and brave. I didn't think it worked.

'Well for a start there are enough chuckerns round here without having to go down to the river at all.' Jenna was obviously going to be positive.

There were a few birds near our cave but they wouldn't last long. If we couldn't find something else to eat then it would be easy for Zach to do whatever he wanted, and I was sure he'd want to do something painful to me. We needed to have our own plan, but Jack broke in before I could say anything, good job because I didn't have a plan anyway.

'We need to ambush them if they come up here to do what

they said.' Jack looked around to see if people were listening, they were. 'I'm assuming we're not going to send Emma down to them?'

Emma looked terrified. Most of us were nodding, but the other younger ones looked unsure.

'One of the things Mary and I have been doing ...' Jack looked at Mary who nodded, 'It's not perfect so we weren't going to tell you until we'd got it right. But we've been making these ...'

Jack walked to the back of the cave, and I was surprised to see his limp had nearly gone, returning and saying, '... bows and arrows.'

Jack and Mary were both looking proud of this invention. They'd made bow strings from dried chuckern guts. Maybe it would work but the arrows weren't very straight and the whole idea looked a little crazy. But Jack got everyone making more of them, then setting up ambush points. At least it gave them something to do. It's what adults would have done, like Jenna said about the grave.

While they did that I spoke to Matt and Ivy: Matt being the biggest, even if he was a bit slow, and Ivy because I thought she was crazy enough to attack anyone. If Zach really was going to try and burn us out then he'd have to come up the slope to our cave. I suggested we just ran at them and did as much damage as we could.

'Better than being burnt alive,' I said to Ivy's grim face.

'The other thing we must do,' Jenna had been taking stock of the food we had and catching a few chuckerns from the bushes, 'we've got to make sure we know where everyone is. If Zach catches someone on their own he'll use it against us. So no wandering off.'

'Where's Lisa?' Sam asked and we all looked around.

'Haven't you noticed her wandering off?' Ivy obviously had. 'She's been doing that nearly every morning. She's up to something I guess.'

'I saw her too,' said Matt. 'I tried to follow her once but she turned on me.'

Matt was always trying to follow Lisa. She didn't like it, he didn't get it.

'Why didn't you say?' Jenna barked at them.

'Why should I? What's it to anyone? She's not found a way back home, I'm sure.' Ivy wasn't going to let Jenna tell her off.

'But ...' Jenna was really cross.

'But what? Does it matter what she's doing?'

'It does now. We need to go and find her.'

Ivy just shrugged.

'She's only away for a little while. She goes down by the river. Near where we've found the rock pools, near the waterfall,' Sara said.

'So you knew she'd been going off as well?' demanded Jenna.

'Sorry.' Sara looked more worried than Ivy. But I could see Ivy's point. It didn't really matter what anyone did. It wasn't exactly as though we had to answer to anyone. That was until Zach had taken to savagery.

No one felt like going to look for Lisa. Jenna tried to persuade me but I didn't like the idea of us splitting up. Zach's lot were probably spying on us. So most of the group carried on with Jack's ambush plans.

I ended up sitting with Jenna and talking about my home stuff. It didn't seem to matter anymore, but I still couldn't get it out of my mind.

'They're really going to throw you out?' Jenna had heard most of it before but still tried to sound surprised.

'Well they will if we ever get out of here.'

'Can they do that, just chuck you out?' Jenna said.

'Seems so, when I'm sixteen. They say with Dad and my brother inside for years and Mum off with this bloke, they don't see why they should look after another Carter.'

'So your aunt and uncle aren't in the same business?'

'What, drugs? Definitely not! They've never got on with us – can't blame them. I got dumped with them because there's no one else.' I poked the ground with a piece of stick. I think it was one of the arrows. It broke.

'There must be someone who can help.'

I shrugged at Jenna's idea. 'And I didn't tell you but I think I saw that Tregarthur woman talking to my aunt.'

'WHAT! Why didn't you tell me?'

'I've no idea if it meant anything.' I tried to calm her down. 'It might explain why my aunt and uncle were so keen to send me on this walk.'

Jenna didn't look any calmer. We didn't have more time to talk about it because Lisa did come back. She wasn't on her own.

'What's that?' Jack jumped up, pointing.

Behind Lisa was a caveman, or actually a cavewoman. Short, hairy, swinging arms but walking. In front of her, Lisa carried a small furry bundle.

'Neanderthal,' said Mary and Jack nodded as we watched the three of them coming up the slope. I had no idea if they were right, it just looked too weird. But I was getting used to weird.

Lisa looked happy, smiling. Now we could see the bundle she

carried was a baby. She didn't look happy for long.

Zach and his lot had been hiding in the bushes, watching and waiting for us. Lisa didn't see them until it was too late.

Zach leapt from the bush, eyes wild and his club swinging. He was on them in seconds but watching it felt as though it happened in slow motion. Zach smashed his club down on the cavewoman's head. We even heard the crack. The Neanderthal, or whatever she was, turned, dazed, baring her teeth. Zach lashed out again. He must have smashed her skull. As she sank to the ground the bundle Lisa was carrying jumped out of her arms and ran to the body of what was her mother. Lisa went berserk. She threw herself on Zach, kicking biting gouging. It took all of his lot to drag her off. Even then she was still fighting and sobbing when the rest of us arrived. We stood back. Lisa fought her way to the baby, who was still pawing at her mother.

So there we were. Zach and his group of six on one side, me with a strange group of less than brave kids on the other. Between us the dead body of the cavewoman, her baby and Lisa.

'I thought that cave-thing was going to attack,' Zach half screeched as though he'd done the right thing. But he had wildness in his eyes: 'That's what you'll all get if you don't do what I say.'

The others around him looked a bit scared. It would have been a good time to take them apart. But I felt sick at what had happened. It looked like murder. Zach was a killer. That wasn't going to make him change into anything but worse.

'Zach,' I said with as much force as I could. 'Zach, just go back to your hole, now.'

I saw Zach looking as though he would challenge me, but the others were already backing away. Soon he would be alone.

I saw his face change, fear replacing his bravery. He turned and they disappeared into the wood.

Then the baby looked up from her dead mother. Her great brown eyes stared at us, helpless. Lisa moved and cradled the small creature. Jenna went forwards and put her arms round them both.

'I was coming to tell you,' Lisa said with tearful eyes.

Then Lisa gave us the whole story. She'd been down at the rock pools on her own one day when Trog, as she called the cavewoman, appeared.

'She seemed to like the name I gave her, and Zog for her baby girl,' Lisa said patting the little one.

'Weren't you scared?' asked Stevie who had been staring at the dead body.

'Yes,' said Lisa. 'But she was really friendly, brought me some berries to eat. Each day we sat and played with Zog.'

'Why didn't you tell us?' Jenna asked more tenderly than she had before.

'I know I should have, it's just they somehow made me feel better. I can't take this place much longer. I know it wasn't right but ...'

I couldn't understand why Lisa meeting up with a cavewoman and playing with her baby should seem right – but it did. I guess in this place you had to just accept what happened. But we couldn't do that with Zach, couldn't accept what he'd done.

'Where did she come from?' I asked.

'Somewhere down by the waterfall.' Lisa stood up holding Zog.

I guessed that we had seen signs of Trog before, hiding in the bushes. The first day I went down to the waterfall and heard something. That was probably Trog and maybe she wasn't on her own. Perhaps I'd not seemed as friendly as Lisa, so she'd stayed hidden.

'Did you see any more of them?' It seemed unlikely to me that she was the only one. There must have been a father to the child. What would happen if he turned up with a lot more of them and found we killed her?

'There weren't any more. I think Trog might have been left behind.'

'If we can sort out Zach we need to go and look,' Jenna said putting her hands on her hips, her taking charge position. 'If there are more then they might know something useful about this place.'

'That's what I thought,' sobbed Lisa. 'In case there were more. That's why we were coming to tell you. Now I wish I'd never planned to tell anyone.' Lisa looked down at the dead body. 'But we're going to have to find something to feed Zog. She was just starting to eat fruit, so she'll have to manage on that. There isn't any milk.'

'Someone's going to have to bury ... to bury,' Jenna seemed unsure whether to use her name.

'Trog,' said Lisa.

'Yes, Trog.' Jenna turned to me, 'Alvin?'

I stepped forward and Matt followed. We had become the official burying party. We lifted the body, carrying it down towards the grave of Other-Sara. Later Trog had a grave stone and flowers, but today we just covered her up with whatever we could find.

When we got back to the cave Zog had already started playing with anything and anyone she could find. She didn't seem to understand that her mother had died. I wondered if that would last. Lisa was trying to feed her berries, but she was much more interested in Jack and Mary's pottery. They were trying to keep her away from the better bits.

The idea of the ambush seemed to have vanished. I didn't think it would have worked so I just made sure that Matt and Ivy knew to stay near me. I asked Sam to stay at the cave entrance and to shout if anyone appeared. Later Jenna swapped with him. But Zach didn't appear. Several of us took turns to keep watch. I wanted to check down by the waterfall to see if there were any more cavepeople, but that wasn't a good idea with Zach still wandering about.

I was there most of the night. I was there when one of Zach's group, or actually one of Demelza's hangers-on, came creeping out of the forest alone in the early morning.

'It's just me – Zoe,' she called. 'There's no one else,' she added as she saw me stand up with my own club in my hand.

-8-

BREAK-UP

'They've gone,' Zoe said in a flat tone.

I knew nothing about Zoe. I didn't even know her name until then. I'd seen her as one of Demelza's lot. Someone to forget.

'Just stay where you are and tell me what you have to say.' I didn't trust her or any of them.

'I hid when they left. I guess they'd gone before they missed me. And I ran off into the bushes. I've been there most of the night,' she said and looked nervous.

Our voices brought everyone else out of the cave. Zoe just moved up to me. There didn't seem to be anyone with her.

'Gone where?' asked Jenna, probably a bit cross that I had even started talking to Zoe on my own.

'When you sent us away.' Zoe looked at me. 'Zach was completely wild. He said he'd come up and club you all to death in your sleep. He knew you'd be waiting tonight. His idea was to keep sending someone up to scare you, wake you up, soften you up. Then when you were all exhausted he'd creep up in the dark and batter you to death.' Zoe choked on her words.

'Good plan,' I said thinking it would have worked. I got a lot of black looks though.

'We were scared of him. I thought he might want a bit of

practice with his club and start on me. Maybe Ryan thought the same. Anyway he persuaded Zach that we should go down to the river and see if there were any more cavemen. That seemed to frighten Zach but he'd set himself up as a conquering hero so he couldn't say he was scared of anything – which he was.'

'So how did you know where to go?'

'Zach made one of us follow you when Lisa came back here. We heard all about her story. So we went down to the river. We couldn't find where she'd lived, but Ryan climbed up on a huge tree that had fallen into the waterfall. And he found a ledge that runs across behind the water. It comes out on the other side.'

'Good of you all to come back and tell us,' Jenna snarled.

'Zach said it must be the way home. He said you all deserved to rot here forever.'

'Why didn't you go?' I wondered if Zach was right and this was the way out.

'I didn't believe him.' Zoe gave me another look. I thought she was trying to get my sympathy. It didn't work. She'd still been one of the girls demanding water when Jenna had been hit.

'Go on,' I said.

'Why would it be any better over there?' she waved her arm in the direction of the waterfall. 'You can see there's nothing there. Zach said he'd make for the mountains. He wouldn't listen to anyone. Just shouting and waving his club. I had to get away.'

There was more but I gave up listening. I was thinking; mostly thinking that we'd got rid of Zach and we didn't want him back. But where had he gone, was there something?

'I'm going down there. Down to the waterfall. Matt, Sam.' I interrupted Zoe, stood up and led them out of the cave. Gone were all my worries about making suggestions. This needed leadership and until someone better came along I was going to do it. Maybe not having Zach there helped though.

'You will come back?' Jenna shouted after me as she stood at the mouth of the cave. I gave her a smile.

We found the tree. Standing on the trunk gave a better view of the grassy plain on the other side of the river. Matt pointed out a herd of animals. Sam said they were deer and I could see him chopping them up in his mind. We looked around for signs of where Trog had lived but didn't find them or signs of any more cavepeople.

We climbed over the tree and found the ledge. By that time Stevie had joined us and was asking lots of annoying questions including: 'Do you think killing Trog would count as murder?'

I didn't know the answer. Did murder only apply to humans? Was Trog human? Lisa said she didn't talk, just grunted. Too difficult a question for me.

We crossed the ledge. It went right behind the waterfall. Stevie nearly fell in when a bird flew out through the spray.

'There's nothing there,' I told the others when we got back to the cave.

'I suppose we saw there was nothing when you and I climbed up to the top of the muffin hill,' said Mary and Jenna gave her a very dark look.

'That's right,' I went on quickly, 'the trees stop, then it's just humpy grass for miles; more forest in the distance and then miles away the mountains you can see from here.'

'So where's Zach going?' asked Jack who was still trying to make straight arrows by chipping away at some wood with a piece of flint.

'He said the mountains,' Zoe chipped in.

'But I can't see why.' I'd no idea what might have been in Zach's mind, apart from nasty craziness. 'And I don't see any point in following him.'

'Maybe Zach will come back.' Sam sounded worried.

'Maybe he will, but I didn't see any sign of him.' I turned to Zoe. 'You're not making this up? It's not just some plot of his and he comes up here tonight to set fire to us?'

Zoe burst into tears and through her sobbing seemed to be saying no. I didn't think she was a good enough liar to make this up, so I believed her. Jenna seemed to as well and she was better at working people out than me.

'Shouldn't we follow him? Just in case,' Jack suggested and I knew that meant his leg was fine now.

'Could do, but why? I don't really feel I want to see much more of him,' I said. 'We just have to hope that if they find something they let us know.'

'Unlikely,' Jenna said.

'Maybe Zach wouldn't, but one of the others might.' I didn't quite know why I was so reluctant to cross the river. Maybe it was because the space over there looked so huge. I was a city boy. I'd found the moor walk bad enough, but all that empty grassland was scary.

No one else was prepared to lead us across the river. I seemed to have taken over, although I felt it was Jenna who made the real decisions. She didn't seem keen on chasing after Zach either.

'If there aren't any more Trogs here, then where did she come from?' asked Stevie.

'Perhaps she got left behind as Lisa suggested,' I said. 'Maybe she couldn't keep up because of Zog.'

'Do you think this has something to do with what that teacher was on about?' said Jack.

'Don't know, but Trog and Zog aren't male so she wasn't talking about them.' I was a bit touchy talking about the teacher. I felt as though she was something to do with me, although I had no idea why.

In the end we gave up talking about it. We didn't follow Zach and we carried on trying to survive.

Surviving was easier without the threat of death from Zach. Jack and Mary led the drive to make things, find things, invent things.

Sam and Ivy took over the chuckern hunting. One day Jack persuaded us to try to catch a deer across the river. All of us had been over the other side. It wasn't just me who found that difficult – although Mary reckoned I had agoraphobia and that's why I didn't like it. Jenna said that was stupid but the two of them had never got on since my night away with Mary.

And Jenna and I seemed to be spending more time together. She was doing the organisation, keeping stocks of food, making sure we had enough wood, asking me what I was going to do each day.

On the deer hunt day we were over the river with me trying to cure my not-agoraphobia. Jack had made a rope from creepers and a noose at the end. He'd been watching what the deer ate and collected a pile of tasty looking leaves. He put them in a pile over the noose and stood back.

'The deer bends down to eat the food, you pull quickly and the noose goes over its neck. Then you two run up and stun it with your club,' Jack said.

It sounded good although I didn't think it would work. It

did, although the first deer was so large that it broke the creeper and ran off. Several more attempts failed until eventually a smaller animal took the bait. Ivy got to the animal first and I was really impressed when she felled the beast with one huge blow. If Zach did come back I wanted Ivy on my side. I was even more astonished when Sam whipped out a piece of flint and slit the animal's throat. There was blood everywhere. Sam looked pleased but I'm sure someone passed out. We carried the deer back. Sam and Ivy chopped it up and we had several days of roast venison before the thing went bad.

That's when Jack came up with the idea of smoking meat. We'd caught another deer. Jack lit a fire in one of the smaller caves and closed off the entrance. He hung the meat over the fire and put a pile of green bushes on the flames. After a lot of choking he seemed to think it had worked. It didn't taste too good but it lasted longer.

Mary used the deer skins to make things. She was drying them out in the sun then washing them in the river, bashing them with stones. She had us all at it. Then we had something to repair our clothes and shoes. She made needles from the deer bones.

'How do they know all this stuff?' I said to Jenna one night when we were sitting outside the cave watching the sunset. Somehow I seemed to be holding her hand at the time.

'I think it's called school,' she said and with the sunset so beautiful her words seemed to end with a kiss. We were both a bit embarrassed but it seemed right.

'So you don't fancy Mary?' she said afterwards.

'Course not.' And I think she believed me, I think I believed me.

The pottery making got better. Instead of burning chuckerns over the fire we made stews. Ivy found lots of herbs. I wondered if they were safe. But when Lisa wasn't looking we tried the stew out on Zog first. She survived, so we ate it. Lisa would have gone wild if she knew we were using Zog for that. She was heavily over-protective of the new baby.

The younger ones weren't too brave about going over the river. No one had any idea whether there were dangerous animals around. We hadn't seen any mammoths nearby. Stevie thought he saw a snake, although I think it was a stick, but eventually they went off together and came back with armfuls of something that looked like wheat or barley, anyway that's what Ivy thought it was. We didn't have to wait to try it out on Zog. She leapt at it. Ivy pounded the stuff up and, having baked it on one of Jack's plates, she made genuine biscuits.

On another night sitting with Jenna she said, 'It's Ok here, isn't it?'

I muttered something.

'I mean now Zach's gone there's no arguments. It's better than home.'

'It's the only home I actually have,' I replied.

'Maybe that's why Miss Tregarthur brought you here.'

'Could be.' I had wondered about that. 'But do you think we're stuck here forever?'

Jenna shrugged. 'Do you think we should go after Zach? It's been a load of Ivy's scratches since they left.' Jenna referred to the passing of time marked by Ivy on the cave wall.

'No idea,' I said. 'I still think if there's any way back it's got to involve this cave and the tunnel. I can't see any point in going anywhere else.'

'So the agoraphobia is still bad.' She laughed at me. Then we went back into the cave. We ended up playing some truth or dare game that Jenna organised. While that went on, Jack and Mary were making more pottery bowls, Matt doing something with deer antlers, and Lisa playing with Zog. Then a gust of wind whipped up the ashes from the fire and through the dusty haze a figure appeared. Ryan stumbled through the cave entrance and fell to the ground.

RYAN'S STORY

I stared at the quivering body lying on the cave floor in the flickering shadows of the fire. Blood streaks ran from a massive black scab on Ryan's forehead. Swelling had closed his left eye. The few remains of his clothes hung in shreds. Deep scratches covered his arms and legs, his ribs stuck out like twigs from his thin body. He gasped as he tried to speak, but his words made no sense.

Jenna was the first to help him, giving him sips of water. He calmed down as she held him. Ryan slipped into a shallow sleep. From time to time he twitched and screamed. He said nothing sensible until the following day.

'It went alright at first,' Ryan's voice became a little stronger. 'We walked for miles on the first day across the plain, then into the forest. Under the trees, the bushes were covered in thorns and we started to get cut and scratched. Some of the cuts burnt as though they were poisoned. Demelza was a real pain and wanted to go back, but Z … Zach wouldn't let anyone go.' Ryan seemed to find it hard to use Zach's name.

'Didn't Demelza want to go?' I said.

'She did – she said it would be a laugh.' Ryan looked up. 'But when it stopped being a laugh, she started whining.'

'Zach made her stay?' I didn't understand why Zach would have put up with Demelza whining.

'He'd been weird since he killed that Trog-thing. I think he'd started to go crazy even then ...' Ryan stopped as though frightened by his own words.

'Then what?' Jack asked impatiently and Ryan went on.

'We heard a lot of strange animal noises and saw herds of deer. One deer had been killed by something – we saw its half-eaten body. Then after we'd been bashing through the bushes for ages it seemed to get easier and I guess we'd started following some sort of trail. We just followed it without thinking how it had been made. Anyway, the trail led us towards the mountains you can see from here.' Ryan gave a vague wave of his arm.

'It started to get dark so we made a sort of camp. Nothing happened that night, but we heard terrible noises nearby. We didn't sleep much. Zach spent most of the night walking up and down swinging his club.' Ryan let out a small gasp. He sat up, took some more water and tried to move, but his face twisted with pain and he fell back. We had to wait, while he recovered enough strength to continue.

'The next day we decided, or Zach decided, we should climb the nearest mountain so we could see further. The only way up meant following a stream. At least we had water but it was hard, steep and slow. We were only, maybe, half way up by the end of the day. Zach found a cave. A damp cave that smelt really awful. We lit a fire.' Ryan turned to Jack. 'I'd had taken back my lighter.'

Jack nodded. 'I wasn't sure when you'd taken it.'

'Haven't got it anymore,' Ryan said and put his hands on the remains of his trousers as though searching.

We waited.

Ryan went on, 'We ate berries and cooked some animal that Zach had killed earlier, it tasted disgusting and Demelza kept on about everything. Zach didn't seem to know what to do with her. I suppose it had been like that even before we left, but every time Demelza wanted something it had to be done.'

'Like what?' I asked and Jenna gave me an exasperated look.

'Like if she wanted water, we'd have to run and get her some. If she wanted to sit down, we had to find her something to sit on. If she got hungry, Zach made me run off into the forest to find more berries.'

'He'd got it really bad for her then!' Jenna said.

'Like slaves?' Stevie asked in a hushed whisper.

Ryan didn't seem to hear Stevie, or took no notice and carried on, 'Demelza started arguing, something stupid about who should sleep where, as if it mattered. The cave stank. All around there were bones and bits of dead animal. The bits made the smell. Anyway I couldn't see why Demelza needed to argue about where to sleep. Should have kept quiet, but I told her to shut up.'

Ryan stopped again, looked around as though he almost expected to see Zach again, and his voice trembled. 'Zach went berserk, screaming and yelling. Then he hit me with his club, over and over again. I might have passed out, but if I did he kicked me when I came round. I thought he'd kill me. I think someone said something to him and he stopped kicking and screamed at me to go, picked me up and threw me out of the cave. I begged him to let me stay. I had nowhere to go and I couldn't see anything in the dark.' Ryan gave a sob. 'But he just shouted louder and I guess the others were too scared, or maybe they didn't care.'

Ryan looked around again. No one moved in the cave and no one said anything so Ryan carried on, 'I crawled out of sight. I could still hear Zach shouting. He said he should have killed me like he killed that Trog thing, so I crawled a bit further. Blood ran down my face and I hurt all over, I wanted to get away. It didn't feel safe on that mountain. There were strange scuffling noises and I kept getting a strong smell, a scary smell, if there's such a thing.'

Ryan paused for another drink. Stevie moved to the back of the group.

'There was no light and I was nearly done for. I bumped into a tree and decided that climbing it would be the best thing I could do. I couldn't get far up. It rained. I wedged myself in a fork in the tree, hung on to the branches and hoped. I dozed off a bit, but I worried about falling. Hours went by, the night cleared and the moon shone. It was quiet, very quiet, no sound of anything. It felt as though everything was waiting.'

Ryan paused again, his voice a shaky whisper. 'Then I smelt something at the bottom of my tree. I couldn't see it, but I heard sniffing. I didn't move. I couldn't move. I held on as tight as I could.'

Ryan had grabbed Jenna's arm as he spoke and held it tightly with his bony hand.

'Whatever it was, it just sat there, sniffing. Once, I saw two eyes in the moonlight. Horrible big yellow eyes staring up at me. I must have shivered, the tree shook and I heard this thing scratching at the trunk, as though it was trying to climb up.'

'Then I heard Zach's voice. I thought I'd got quite a long way from the cave but I could hear him shouting. I wondered who he would attack next. It wasn't only me that heard the noise. I could make out the shape of a huge thing as it slipped away from my tree. I knew what would happen, but I couldn't do anything about it. I got out of the tree and even though it hurt, I ran and ran down the hill, smashing into more trees, banging into rocks and falling into the stream. As I ran, I started to hear the screams. That made me run faster. There were more screams. I could hear Demelza's scream, much louder than the others.' Ryan's own voice almost screamed. He stopped, his breathing fast and shallow.

'And?' Jack couldn't wait.

'I must have gone quite a long way because I couldn't hear the screams anymore. I climbed another tree and I think I passed out. I didn't come round until the next day. I got out of the tree, but I hurt too much to go any further. I found a few berries and lay against the tree trunk hoping someone would find me. But of course there isn't anyone. Is there?' Ryan looked at me but I just shook my head.

'The night came again. I felt worse, all hot and cold. I don't know how long I was like that, it must have been days. My head kept hurting. When I slept I thought I could hear that sniffing thing coming for me. I thought I could hear Demelza's screams.' Ryan fell back.

I wondered what had made Demelza scream and worse, what might have made her stop screaming.

Ryan raised himself up on his elbows. 'Then after two, or perhaps three days, I woke up surrounded by Trog-like people. I was too far gone to do anything. They poked me and grunted. I had a silly flash that I was in a film. I think I started laughing in a weird sort of way. Then they copied me and soon they all started this grunt laughing. I thought they were going to eat me, but one of them gave me a drink from some sort of skin bag, it burnt my throat and I don't remember much after that. The next time I came round I guess I was in their camp. There were about ten of them – eating, tearing meat from a dead deer. I think it was dead ... not absolutely certain ... maybe it was still moving a bit. They threw me a piece. I hadn't eaten for days so I ate it. It was warm, but not from cooking.'

Ryan described how he stayed with them and slowly recovered. He watched them hunting. The Trogs chased deer over a cliff near their first camp and then killed them as they lay injured at the bottom. From time to time they gave him bits of food.

Then one day he woke alone.

'They'd vanished. I almost wondered if I had imagined it all. I had no idea where I was, where they'd left me. They'd moved me when they moved their camp and that had happened several times. The trees were so thick that I couldn't see the mountains. I had to guess which way to go. I did find a few berries, nothing else to eat, but there's a lot of water out there – stream after stream. I think I went round in circles for days. At night I hid in any tree I could find. One night I fell out, that's when I hit my head and it started to bleed again. One of the streams led me to our river so I got back. The last problem was getting through whatever you'd put over the ledge.'

'We worried that if one Trog could get over, then others could come,' said Jack.

'In case they found out what we did to the last one,' Jenna said looking at Lisa.

'I thought about trying to swim across. I called out, but no one heard. Eventually I crawled through.' Ryan finished and lay back on the cave floor. His wounds looked bad. I wondered if he would survive. Jenna and Mary tried to make him comfortable, not really possible in a dingy cave I thought.

I went over Ryan's tale in my mind. In the half-taken, half-forced position as leader I knew that a decision had to be made and if I didn't make it then it would hang over us forever.

'We have to go and see if we can find any of them,' I said as if it needed no further discussion.

'B … b … but they're all … dead,' said Jack looking from side to side as if hoping for support from someone.

'You are joking?' Lisa looked at me as though I must be stupid.

'Go looking for Zach?' whispered Ryan. 'Never.'

I wasn't entirely thinking of Zach. I realised that we now had a direction, a way to follow. The hunting ground over the river had always unsettled me but now we could follow the route Zach had taken. It might not lead anywhere but it was somewhere to go. If we found Zach … well then that would be a different thing.

'So we abandon them?' Jenna asked. 'You're all still hoping someone's searching for us, aren't you?'

No one answered.

'So we have to find out if any of them are still alive.'

I knew Jenna had convinced most of the rest of them, but I still heard grumbling comments, whispered in the cave. The decision had been made although I knew I'd have to lead any expedition. So they would all soon just blame me. I sighed and I saw Jenna smile.

'Set me up then.' I grinned back at her.

'Absolutely. Crazy idea. Knew you'd like a challenge.'

-10-

EXPEDITION

Going after Zach took on a different meaning as everyone talked about it. It became bigger, with thoughts of how it might lead to our rescue. No one talked of anything else except the expedition and who would go.

I'd made the suggestion so it was obvious to everyone else that I would be leading it, even if I had other ideas. But I didn't really have any ideas at all. I had worries instead. It seemed tied up with Miss Tregarthur and this promise, which we had no chance of keeping because we couldn't find anyone to save. And why had I now decided to go after the one person who I would have been quite happy to see dead?

Had I set myself up to lead or was it Jenna who'd decided I was the best person to be the leader? More likely I wasn't leader of anything and it was Jenna and she was using me.

It had been raining hard for several scratches – we'd given up calling them by days of the week and went by Ivy's scratches on the cave wall. No one remembered when she started and we didn't know which day it was. Jenna had worked out a sort of rota for doing stuff so the scratches got names, chuckern was the day we did most of the hunting – chuckern scratch, wood scratch made sure we had a pile of burning stuff and so on. Ivy had suggested we should have a burial scratch which would have been awful because it might be needed. As it turned out we hadn't got enough names and Jenna said we needed a rest day.

'Like a Sunday was meant to be,' she'd said, although no one I knew did much resting on a Sunday. Jenna wanted to call it Sunday, but Ivy's burial name was used by most of us.

After my Zach chasing suggestion, and yes my resolution had been repeatedly broken – not to make suggestions – it rained through chuckern, wood, and fruit. But when the sun broke through on burial I was standing outside the cave and up came Jenna, giving me a hug because we'd seriously become an item since that kiss.

'You still going?'

And the way she said it confirmed who was really in charge. Because what she meant was: get on with it, so it didn't need an answer.

'Who are you taking with you?'

Now that had worried me, and I knew that Jenna was going to tell me who I should take, but a little mischief crept in. 'I thought just me and Mary.'

Jenna whacked me on the arm. She was almost going to storm off, but I held her back and eventually she broke into a smile.

'Over my dead body,' she said.

'Well you've picked the right day,' and that got me another vaguely friendly poke.

There was silence then. I was getting used to her ways. Jenna had started this conversation. She was now waiting to see who I'd thought of taking with me. Then she'd decide whether she was going to make changes.

'I might go on my own. It would be less trouble,' I said and we wandered slowly towards the forest.

'Then, when you don't come back, what do we do?' Jenna replied.

'Eh?'

'Suppose Ryan's beast thing gets you, how would we know?' Jenna sounded suddenly angry. 'We wouldn't know what had happened. After a while someone else would follow you and they'd get eaten by the thing. Then someone else – we'd all get killed off.'

'What difference does it make if someone comes with me?'

Jenna put her hand on my shoulder. 'At least one person might get back – like Ryan did.'

'To tell you I'd been eaten?'

'I'd want to know.'

'So I'd better take a fast runner? Someone to get away quick and come and tell you?'

'No – take someone slow. Then the beast gets them first,' Jenna grinned, her anger draining away.

'You want to come then? You're slow enough.'

Jenna punched me again and she laughed. I'd stopped laughing at her punches. This open air life had done great things for her fitness and her figure.

Our walk had taken us towards the two graves. There were fresh flowers. Sara had found some real flowers and used burial day to put new ones on Other-Sara's grave. Lisa did the same for Trog.

'There's room for more graves,' I said.

'That's the sort of thing Ivy would say, except she'd say there was room for all of us.'

'Perhaps she would be right, but you'd have to dig a spare grave so the last person could just fall in.'

'Come on, let's go before you turn into Ivy. I think the rest are waiting to hear your plans.' Jenna turned back.

She was right. The rest stood by the cave entrance, watching. We ran back as the rain started again and everyone sat around the fire. Decisions to be made.

'I'll go,' Jack said trying his best to sound courageous, but hiding his face by bending and poking the ashes.

'Me too,' Matt said puffing out his chest.

I hoped Jenna would help but she just looked at me. But who did I feel should come? How many?

'Maybe we should all go,' said Mary.

'Look what happened last time we all went for a walk.' I tried to laugh, but I had no idea what might be out there. What would happen if we met Ryan's beast? Taking everyone would be too difficult. I'd sort of decided that three would be the right number, or was that what Jenna had said?

Matt was the strongest person although he might not be the quickest. But they'd need someone here if more Trogs arrived, or something worse. They'd need Matt. And Jack? His leg still gave him trouble from time to time even though he tried to hide it.

'Thanks,' I spoke in a tone that I barely recognised as my own. 'I ... we ... can't go until the rain stops and we'll need to take food and anything useful. Any ideas?' I was playing for time and hoping for inspiration.

No one said anything. I suppose they needed to know who would go, the uncertainty made them too anxious to come up with ideas. So I carried on.

'Matt, I think it would be best if you stayed. You're the strongest and you're needed here.'

'I could do with Jack being here ... helping ... he's got lots of

new ideas ... especially a new idea for a water supply ... and ...'
Mary was finding reasons for keeping Jack.

'Mary, I agree!' I interrupted her before the list got longer.
Jack didn't look too upset, but there were more blushes.

'So who is going with you?' Jenna glared at me. 'Who's left?'

'Might as well be me,' Sam said. 'When there's something
awful to do you always pick on me, so I might as well volunteer.'
He walked across the cave and sat next to me.

Sam always did seem to get the worst jobs. But with Zach
gone, he wasn't bullied into doing them. Sam might not have
realised it, but our diet and daily hunting had changed him.
The plump round faced boy had become taller, leaner, and very
much stronger. I liked the idea of Sam coming with me.

Without another word, Ivy moved over and sat next to Sam.

'Ivy?' I looked at her.

'What?'

'You're coming?'

'Looks like it.' The firm lines on Ivy's face showed her
determination.

I'd seen Ivy hunting with Sam and I knew she was fast and
strong, if a little odd and more than a little miserable. I was
happy with these two and Jenna looked as though this had
gone to plan – her plan.

'Who's going to do the hunting here?' asked Stevie who had
joined Ivy and Sam on many occasions, but didn't look as though
he couldn't hunt on his own.

'We think we've got the bow and arrows right now. We want
to try them out for hunting.' Mary beamed and poked Jack.

From behind him, Jack lifted out their newest bow. Jack and
Mary might be good at inventing things but the bow didn't really

look much good, we tried it out – it wasn't. Still, it seemed to stop us talking about going after Zach. And it was definitely better not to talk about the sniffer, as Ryan's beast became called.

'So that's it?' Jenna said. 'Just the three of you?'

'It's what you wanted, isn't it?'

'Me?' Jenna smiled and I knew I was right. I wondered whether she'd spoken to Sam and Ivy before they volunteered.

Jenna carried on making plans, arranging things for us to take. 'Smoked meat, some cooked chuckerns, some of the biscuits, and there are a couple of water bottles left that might be Ok.'

We'd been using Jack and Mary's pots for water. They'd made one large bowl that we filled. It saved going to the river every day – although we really needed more than one water scratch.

Several more scratches passed. I was hesitating.

'What are you waiting for?' Jenna asked one evening. Which I think again meant get on with it. 'You want a sign or something?' She poked me in the ribs to get a response.

I flinched. Jenna's pokes were even worse than her punches. 'I'm just not sure this is worth doing.'

'Probably right, but it's too late now,' Jenna said with a tight lipped face.

'Something might happen here. Something in the tunnel. We might miss it.'

'Ok, then don't go. We'll just eat all the stuff I've got ready.'

Jenna knew how to make it happen. 'Suppose it has to be done then.' I stood and turned to face the cave entrance.

Jenna stared at me.

'What?'

'Are you the same Alvin I went to school with?'

'Are you the same Jenna?' I said before turning and saying in a loud voice: 'Tomorrow we go – that alright Ivy? Sam?' They both gave a slow nod.

The next morning, at the first sign of light, everyone gathered at the waterfall to watch us leave. We took backpacks, or the remains of them half repaired with patches of deer skin. They were loaded up with things Jenna had collected.

Jack handed over his latest bow and some arrows. 'Just in case you meet the sniffer,' he said. He was a lot more confident than I was about his invention.

I told Matt to block the path after we left. Ryan had broken through and we needed to make a much better barrier.

'Something that we can move when we need to get out,' Jack suggested.

'Like a portcullis,' said Stevie. 'You know, like that thing they have in castles to stop people getting in.'

I could see Jack's mind working on Stevie's idea. It might take time. I held up a whistle I'd found at the back of the cave, it had fallen from one of the packs. 'We'll blow the whistle and you can help us across – when we get back.' I wanted the rest to believe that we would return.

Ivy still muttered, 'If we get back.' Loud enough for everyone to hear.

Jenna stepped forward. There were hugs and kisses and tears.

I crossed the ledge and slid down a creeper onto the grassy plain. Sam and Ivy joined me. The rest watched as we started to disappear into the longer grass. I looked back and waved with many thoughts churning in my head. Would we ever return? Would we discover a way home? Would we find out what had happened to Zach and the others? Did we really want to find Zach anyway?

TIGER CAVE

Leaving the waterfall, we crossed the grassy plain where we'd hunted deer, the journey easy and familiar at first. Soon it became harder and slower, with hollows and deep holes making it impossible to take a straight line towards the forest. I'd talked to Ryan, trying to get a clear idea of the route he'd taken with Zach. Ryan still seemed terrified when he talked about it. I didn't think he would ever recover completely.

With every step we could see more detail of the mountains in the distance. Dark jagged peaks formed a black barrier against the sky. Smoke drifted from the top of one massive summit.

'That looks like the volcano they headed for at first.' I pointed ahead. 'Ryan said head for the volcano.'

'I expect it's about to blow up,' suggested Ivy.

I smiled, there was almost something reassuring about Ivy's miserable remarks.

The sun was high in the sky by the time we reached the fringe of the forest. Huge trees topped with leafy canopies let through an eerie green light. Beneath the trees, bushes thick with vicious thorns covered the ground. I searched for the trail that Ryan had followed. We found it.

'Wonder what made this track?' Sam said looking at the well worn route.

'I expect we'll find out soon,' replied Ivy as we followed the trail, the only possible way into the forest.

We walked on in silence. Much later, rounding a bend, we came to a grassy clearing. It looked peaceful and the sun shone. A small stream ran across the trail and we stopped to drink and eat some of the fruit in our packs. Ivy and Sam persuaded me to try the smoked meat.

'Mm ... mm,' was the best comment I could make with my teeth gummed together.

We didn't stop long. It was awfully quiet and we kept looking at the trail.

'I think those are footprints?' Ivy said looking at the softer ground by the stream.

'Could be,' I shrugged.

'Let's get out of this clearing,' said Sam.

'You mean the sniffer's waterhole,' Ivy suggested.

I looked at Sam and rolled my eyes at Ivy's comment. But we went on, slightly faster. The trail turned from the stream and appeared to run towards the mountains.

As the day became hotter, the air under the trees grew stale and sickly. The ground started to rise in a slow steady climb, but the trees were tall and too close together to see very far.

'What's that?' Sam stopped and listened.

We'd been hearing bird calls all the time. Now there was humming coming from ahead. It was getting louder. Nothing like the birds. Much louder.

Ivy was standing in front and saw it first. 'Run,' she cried, and stumbled off the track into the thick forest.

I'd heard of hornets but never seen one, and definitely never seen a swarm of thousands which were buzzing towards us.

I followed Ivy. Sam was a bit slower. He screamed; his back covered in vicious looking yellow insects. I pulled him into a bush. The main swarm had passed. Ivy and I bashed the insects away from him and they took off to follow the rest. Sam's back was covered in stings. He was still screaming.

'We need to get him back to the stream,' Ivy said trying to get Sam to stand. He was in too much pain so we had to carry him.

Back at the clearing Ivy set to bathing the stings. She seemed to know as much as Mary. Ivy often collected plants, not just for putting in our stews, but some she tried out on the frequent bruises and cuts that we all got. Some worked, some did nothing.

'Alvin,' she said and I could see the worry in her face. Sam wasn't looking good. 'Alvin you carry on with this, I need to see if I can find something to put on the stings.'

Ivy disappeared into the bushes leaving me dabbing at Sam's back. He wasn't saying anything and seemed almost unconscious from the shock.

I hoped she'd be back soon but it seemed ages before she returned carrying a huge bundle of leaves. Soaking them in the stream she bashed them to a paste before heaping the sticky green mess on to Sam's back. He yelled. I left her to do it and wandered off. It wasn't late but I didn't think we'd be able to go far with Sam. We might even have to go back. Even so we needed to find somewhere to spend the night and I didn't think either the sniffer waterhole or the track were safe.

Peering through the trees I could see the ground sloped upwards. There wasn't a trail but it looked as though we might be able to get higher up. I went on a bit further. Now I could see I was on a hill. I couldn't see the top but the trees gave way to crags and grass. I went back down.

Sam seemed to be asleep, breathing more easily. The red wheals on his back still looked angry and swollen but maybe a little better. Ivy was still pounding up more leaves.

'Better?' I asked her.

'I doubt it,' she replied and I guess I shouldn't have expected anything positive from her.

'We'll have to move out of here before night.' I knelt down beside her. 'I think we can get up there.' And I pointed to the hill which was just about visible through the trees. 'I suppose we'll have to carry him.'

I must have disturbed Sam and his eyes opened, his face still twisted in pain. 'I'm Ok,' he stuttered, obviously not Ok at all.

'Leave him for a while,' Ivy said and we moved away to let him rest. His eyes closed.

Left alone we had nothing to do except talk. Jenna was the only person I'd told about seeing Miss Tregarthur at my home, talking to my aunt. Now I let Ivy know the whole story. She didn't seem to find it strange at all but then she didn't seem to find anything strange.

'My mum's a white witch,' she told me and explained that was why she knew about herbs and plants. It also explained why odd things didn't seem odd to Ivy. I wanted to ask her why she was so miserable most of the time, but it didn't seem a good idea.

'I guess you want to know why I seem so miserable?'

How did she know that? I stared at her.

'Everyone wants to know, not many ask.'

'Oh.'

'Mum takes it too far,' Ivy went on, and I suppose I looked baffled. 'The witch thing. She thinks we should have some special bond. Goes on and on about it. As though we should be telepathic. It drove dad away in the end. He was the only sane one at home.'

She stopped. I saw her body heave. 'I miss him so much. He won't come back. Won't talk to me. It's just Mum and her daft ideas. I can't escape and sometimes I just can't stand it.'

I think I just kept saying, 'Oh.' But I was getting anxious about time passing. If we had to carry Sam it would take hours to get anywhere up the hill. 'We'll have to wake him,' I said in the end.

Ivy gently removed the pile of leaves from his back and Sam stirred. He was a little better. We propped him up and gave him water. He tried to stand, but we both had to hold him and that's how we set off. I knew he was still in awful pain but Sam was a stronger person than I'd realised. It wasn't long before he tried to walk on his own, stumbling but still moving, and we slowly made our way upwards.

As we rose higher I thought it looked like we were on a solitary peak. It rose through the forest, quite a distance from the main range of mountains. Climbing even higher the few trees that clung to the rock looked dead, with cracked sun bleached branches. By the time we reached the top it was early evening and not light enough to make out much detail in the forest below, but we were above the treetops and could see the last rays of the sun setting over the distant peaks.

'I think we should stop here for the night.' I pointed to a rock ledge, below the top of the hill. It would provide some shelter.

Sam collapsed on the grass. He wasn't moving or talking. Ivy had brought some of her leaf mixture and she spread more on to his back. The stings were less angry but Sam was exhausted by the climb. We tried to make him comfortable.

'At least this feels safer than the trail,' I said as Ivy and I ate some of our food and looked at Sam. I could see that Ivy was thinking of something awful to say, so I said, 'Unless you think there are monster eagles that will swoop down and rip us to pieces?'

'Don't be stupid,' replied Ivy. 'It would be pterodactyls.' She turned away and I half-wondered if Ivy had just made a joke.

'There aren't pterodactyls ... are there?' Sam muttered drowsily. I thought that must be a good sign.

'A fire would be good,' I said. I think we were quite high up and it felt colder.

'No problem.' Ivy had brought along pieces of flint, moss and sticks in her pack. 'Matt showed me how to start a fire.'

I broke up some pieces of dead wood. After several attempts, Ivy made a spark by hitting the flints together and the fire started to burn.

'Might even keep animals away,' I said.

'Not Ryan's beast,' replied Ivy.

I really thought I'd seen a smile on Ivy's face but it was difficult to be sure because it was nearly dark. I lay down, using my backpack as a pillow with an 'ouch' before I took out the arrows.

It was a quiet night on the hill. Sam didn't stir and the only noises were the scufflings we had grown used to hearing. When I woke the sun was up burning off the early morning mist over the forest treetops. The small patches of grass that grew between the rocks were wet with dew. Sam was sitting up.

'Better?' I asked.

'Fine,' he replied but I wasn't so sure. I took him some water. As I did we suddenly heard a thunderous roar.

'What was that?' Sam cried.

'It's coming from the other side of the hill,' I said.

'Up here!' Ivy called in a hushed voice and waved to us. She must have woken earlier and now she lay on her front, looking over the top of the hill.

I crept up to her. Sam followed slowly.

Ivy waved her arm and hissed, 'Stay down. Stay down.'

Last night it had been too dark to see, but over the top of the hill the ground sloped down to a large open green area dotted with small trees and bushes; edged with cliffs that fell away in the distance. One large tree stood alone and near this a huge mammoth roared and charged backwards and forwards. Chasing it were ten or more hairy men, screaming and grunting and howling and waving clubs. The men looked a bit like Trog, but taller and had skins tied around their waists. The terrified mammoth rushed from side to side trying to escape the noise and men. Finally the mammoth raced across the plain and disappeared over the edge, along with a huge howl from the cavemen.

'I've seen a movie about this ... or read a book ... or something,' Ivy mumbled.

'Is this all a film?' I wondered.

'So that's how you catch a mammoth,' Sam said bravely.

The group of men followed the mammoth, scrambling over the cliff edge and slowly disappeared. Silence returned as we stared at the empty space below.

'It's too much – mammoths, cavemen, sniffers.' Sam put his head in his hands, bravery deserting him. 'How are we ever going to survive in this?'

'Probably won't ...'

'Ivy, please!' I didn't think that needed saying. 'Sam do you think you can go on? Or do we need to go back.'

Sam got to his feet. 'Go on.'

We ate a little and then clambered down the rocky hill only needing to help Sam from time to time although I could see he was still in pain. We made our way back to the track.

'I hadn't really believed you ... about the mammoths,' said Ivy.

'Me neither,' added Sam.

'This has got to have some connection to Miss Tregarthur,' I said, stopping and leaning against a tree.

'What was she doing here? Something disgusting I expect.' Ivy spoke her thoughts aloud.

'How did she get here?' Sam seemed to be thinking similar thoughts. 'And how did she get back?'

'I think it was all a plan to come back here and I think she planned to bring us with her,' Ivy said firmly. 'From what you told me yesterday I think that all fits.'

'What did Alvin tell you yesterday?' Sam asked.

'Tell you later. We need to get on.' I tried to set off but Ivy stopped me.

'That teacher was worse than weird,' she said. 'Some of the younger ones said she gets nasty. I think it was Sara who said there were stories ...'

'Yeah, stories and this feels like one. But this promise must have something to do with saving someone.' I moved off.

'Could be her dad? Didn't her note say something about her dad being really ill? Maybe he's the one who needs saving,' Sam added as he followed me.

'Why would she think we could save her dad?' I snapped. 'I mean what use would a group of crazy kids be to some sick old man?'

Sam looked away.

'What happened to those two women who were supposed to be helping? Someone's mothers I think,' Ivy said.

'They just seemed to disappear when the rain started,' I replied. 'Somehow all that seems just as unreal as it does here. Every time I try and think about things before – home or anything, it seems a bit blurred.'

The other two agreed with me.

'I guess we just push on.' I went for the trail – to search for the cave, wondering what else we might find.

Ryan said that the trail ended at the base of the foothills. 'Just follow the stream after that.'

The thick trees and plants started to thin out as we climbed again. I couldn't see any trees at all on the peaks, only bare black rock. The mountains looked bleak and unfriendly. Even on this warm day a ring of mist swirled around the summits. We were soon out of breath and high enough to look back towards the hill where we'd spent the previous night.

'We must keep going. We don't want to be stuck here, like Zach, when it gets dark,' I called to Sam who was lagging behind with Ivy staying with him. I could see it was difficult for him but we might not be safe here. I looked on up ahead. 'That might be the cave,' I said, waiting as the other two caught up.

The dark patch became an obvious opening as we climbed further.

'Should we go round to the side first, in case the sniffer is in there?' Sam stopped and shuffled.

I nodded and we walked around, looking up for any sign of movement against the dark opening. Getting closer, a slow step at a time, I fingered the bow Jack had given me. I wasn't sure it would be any use. I stopped and listened. It all seemed so quiet. I moved forward. Ivy and Sam stopped as I inched towards a pillar of rock that marked the entrance to the cave. Holding on to the rock I peered in – it was too dark to see what lay inside. I drew an arrow from my pack and held the bow half drawn.

'Stay there,' I whispered, but Sam and Ivy didn't look as though they were going anywhere.

My heart pounded as I took a few more slow steps. I looked back over my shoulder at the other two, decided I had to go for it and stepped into the shadows. It was much colder and I shivered and waited for my eyes to grow accustomed to the dark. There was a sound of scuffling coming from the deepest corners of the cave. I stopped and the scuffling stopped. I took another step. Something leapt from behind a pile of small rocks and rushed towards me.

I fired off an arrow and fled, shouting, 'Run!'

I collided with the other two before they had time to move and we all fell in a heap as we were overtaken by several, very small, animals that fled out of the cave and disappeared down the hillside.

'What were they?' said a pale and shaking Sam.

'They looked like guinea pigs.' I felt really stupid having been driven out of the cave by such small creatures.

'I expect the bigger ones will be along soon,' said Ivy.

'Are the bigger ones still inside?' Sam didn't move.

'Don't think so,' I said going back through the entrance.

The cave was damp and rank with a strange smell. Water seeped through the roof and fell into a pool on the sandy floor, making a dripping sound, but apart from that it was quiet in the cave, no more scuffling. There was nothing alive left in the cave.

'Maybe these are mammoth bones,' said Sam picking up a huge piece out of the sand.

'Those aren't.' Ivy pointed to a skull. She discovered more bones in the sand.

'These must be their packs.' I picked up the remains of back-packs from the back of the cave. They had been ripped to shreds.

'Can we go?' Sam trembled.

'What happened?' wondered Ivy.

'There's more than one skull,' I said poking the bones with my foot.

The cave seemed even quieter, just the occasional drip of water.

'Let's get out ... come on,' stuttered Sam. 'It'll be back soon.'

'I think the sniffing thing got them,' I said. 'But I don't think it can have been here for a while, there's no fresh meat.'

I shuddered as I looked at the bones – bones probably belonging to someone we knew, bones that had been chewed by animals, one of which might return at any moment.

'That could be blood.' Ivy pointed to a large stain on the sandy floor, lit by a ray of sunshine penetrating the dark.

I stared around the cave, looking at the bones, the blood and the torn backpacks. 'I can't work this out ... that's Zach's club ...' I pointed at a broken branch in the corner of the cave. Zach had carved notches in the wood.

'And there's this.' Sam held up Ryan's lighter, which he had found partly buried in the sand.

'But I can only find three skulls.' I couldn't follow this. 'Maybe someone escaped.'

'But how?' Sam moved nearer to the entrance.

'Impossible to work that out, but I agree with Sam that we should get out of here.' Sam looked relieved until I said, 'But I want to go further up the mountain.'

'Why?' was Sam's shrill reply. 'Haven't we found what we've been looking for?'

'We need to be certain. See if anyone did escape.' I set my face hard, I didn't want any discussion.

We left the cave and continued to climb. As the light faded, we'd nearly reached the rocky crags of the summit. We stopped under another rock overhang.

'I've only got berries left,' said Sam looking into his backpack. Sam was looking much better despite the long climb.

'Me too,' replied Ivy. 'We finished off the chuckerns last night.'

'I've still got some smoked meat,' I said tearing off two pieces from a chunk I had in my pack. 'Not sure how you tell when this stuff is rotten.' I sniffed the pieces and screwed up my nose, before throwing some to the other two. Despite the smell we all ended up chewing lumps of smoked meat.

That night up on the mountain, above the trees, we felt the cold. We hadn't carried any wood with us and couldn't light a fire so we huddled together and waited for dawn. I didn't think going back to the sniffer cave was a good idea.

As the light slowly appeared, we moved on and soon could see over the top of the mountain and into the distance. Standing in silence we saw a vast dark landscape of trees beneath us. There were no familiar towns or houses; only more trees. We watched as the sun rose, bringing colour to the landscape, but seeing nearly only one colour – green. In the far distance I thought I might be able to see the sea. The mist hanging over miles and miles of forest made it difficult to be certain.

'Nothing.' I sat heavily on the ground. I'd believed there might be something, something that would show us signs of human life.

'Wait! There's something down there.' Sam pointed down the mountain.

'Anyone selling pizza?' I said but didn't get up.

'Don't expect they deliver,' added Ivy.

'No, you look, down there, huts. Look.'

I jumped up. 'And people,' I said as I shaded my eyes and stared.

'They must be the ones who killed the mammoth,' said Ivy. 'I'm not sure if they would help us. More likely they would chase us over a cliff as well.'

'I still want to go down and have a look. We've got to see. This may be the answer. Let's go – but quietly. We want to get a close look at them before they see us.'

The other two looked doubtful, but they followed – keeping as quiet as possible. Lower down, the trees and bushes grew again and we tried to keep hidden. The mammoth hunters had looked wild and savage.

By the time we reached the bottom of the mountain the weather had changed. The sky darkened as clouds gathered behind us and wind rustled the trees. We crept through the bushes keeping the huts in sight.

'Keep down,' I said in a hushed whisper, crouching behind a prickly bush and waving at the other two to do the same.

We were now close enough to see people walking around the circle of primitive huts. The people looked like the mammoth hunters, except they were all women.

'Where are the men?' Sam stared with his mouth wide open

– some of the women wore bits of skins, but few of them wore much in the way of clothing.

'Isn't that Demelza?' I pointed to one of the figures.

'I think it is,' Sam replied, his mouth still open.

'Do you think they're going to eat her?' Ivy's eyes opened nearly as wide as Sam's mouth although I thought that Ivy didn't sound too concerned.

'Are we going to try and get her out of there?' Sam said while sinking lower behind the bush.

'Not sure if she has been captured, she's not tied up and I think she's doing something.' I pointed. Demelza seemed to be grinding something with a stone. 'Maybe she was rescued.'

'How do we find out?' Sam shuffled and looked nervous.

'I think that'll be simple – we ask them.' I tapped Sam on the shoulder indicating to him to turn around.

A crowd of short, hairy cavemen with very large clubs had silently gathered behind us. My first thought was that we were going to die, but my second thought came quickly, 'What is that terrible smell?'

-12-

CROW

Against the blackening sky one caveman stood out. With his club raised he advanced, taller, hairier and even smellier than the rest. A huge furry animal skin added to the caveman's hairiness and smelliness. The flattened skin draped over his shoulders with huge paws tied together in front. The animal's head hung over his back with two sharp curved tusks sticking out from its open mouth.

The caveman looked us up and down, or as Ivy said later, 'wondering how to cook us'. Then he pointed at the bow I carried, opened his mouth wide and roared: 'Haarfer.' The rest joined in, stamping their feet and howling the word, 'Haarfer.'

Escape was impossible as their leader wrapped me in a hug. The others cheered, a cheer mixed with a grunt and a spray of spit. Ivy and Sam were standing absolutely rigid, but were wrapped up in smelly hairy hugs as all the cavemen embraced us.

Hugs over, I looked at the surrounding group. These were the cavemen we'd seen chasing the mammoth. Taller and more upright than the Trog Zach had killed. They had long straggly ginger hair and beards, each one had some covering made of skin. Parts of their bodies were painted in blue and red colours. Some had necklaces made of bone.

The Stinkers, the name Sam gave to our new friends, waved

and pushed us towards their huts. We stepped into a flattened mud circle surrounded by flimsy looking buildings made of reeds and branches. As we did the first few drops of rain started to fall and within seconds, torrents of water poured from the dark sky. The wind howled. The Stinkers ran around joining in the howling. Their leader, with the animal cloak, pushed us into a slightly larger hut.

Inside the hut Demelza sat cross legged, holding a stone and grinding some kind of grain against a piece of wood. She looked a mess. Her hair, previously long, dark and glossy from using the most expensive products, now stuck to her head with dirt and yellow grease. She wore a skin, which covered only some of her and its half rotten state produced an overpowering stench. Her necklace was one of her only recognisable features. She seemed to take no interest in us.

'Demelza?' I squatted in front of her trying not to breathe in her smell. She looked up at me with blank eyes. After a few seconds she looked away and returned to pounding with her stone. The leader crouched beside her and lifted part of the deer skin to reveal an angry looking wound on her right thigh. Demelza tugged the skin back over her leg.

Then the caveman stood, stabbed at his chest with a finger and howled: 'Cro...oo...ow.'

It sounded a bit like 'Crow' and we decided that must be his name.

He pointed at me and said, 'Haarfer.'

'Actually ...' I felt Sam grab me by the arm.

'Just agree with him. I think 'Haarfer' or whatever he calls you is important.'

'Haarfer!' Crow repeated. He beamed and banged me on the shoulder.

I pointed to the others saying, 'Ivy and Sam'.

Crow couldn't say the names and soon gave up trying. But he gave Ivy a wide grin. I tried again to talk to Demelza but before I could say anything Crow grunted something like, 'Ass.' That sounded like a perfect name for Demelza and she appeared to recognise 'Ass' because she stopped pounding and gave Crow a brief glare.

Crow pointed at the beast's skin over his shoulder, slipped off the cloak and brought the head up towards Demelza. She gave a scream which pierced the air, pierced the storm and brought other Stinkers to stare at us. Crow waved them away. Demelza dropped her stone and cowered against the side of the hut with her hands over her head, sobbing. Crow gave a sort of laugh, put the cloak back on and strode out of the hut, leaving us staring at Demelza.

'I think we've found the sniffing thing,' Ivy said.

'What do you mean?' asked Sam.

'I guess Crow is wearing the remains of it. They must have killed Ryan's sniffer. That's how she escaped.' Ivy knelt down in front of Demelza.

'After it killed Zach and the other two,' I said. 'That's what must have happened in the cave. Killing the beast made all those marks in the sand. It makes sense. Demelza probably watched the beast attacking them and that's when she injured her leg.' I looked down at her and said, 'Hard to imagine – being at school together.'

'You weren't, much,' Ivy said.

Demelza went back to pounding grain, taking no notice of us. Crow returned carrying an animal skin bag that slopped with liquid. It opened at the neck and was bound with twine.

Crow offered it to me, I retched at the smell. Crow laughed and banged me on the arm.

'Got to do it.' Sam pointed at the skin bag. Sam had always learnt to give in rather than resist but this time I thought it was the right decision.

I took a swig, looked away and passed it to Sam without saying anything. My throat burnt and my eyes started streaming. Crow gave another howling laugh. I dodged another slap. Crow just grunted and grinned to show his broken yellow teeth. He made us drink again. It wasn't offered to Demelza or Ivy.

The storm, which had hit so suddenly, disappeared with the same speed. We left the hut and watched the Stinkers repairing damage. Crow's hut had survived mostly intact. The circle of bare earth had become a muddy bog and the Stinkers were covered with the mud.

One hut sat further away from the circle. Two Stinkers were standing outside, looking as though they were guarding something or someone.

Sam seemed to be feeling the effects of the drink. He swayed and collapsed on the ground giggling. Having mended the huts, the Stinker men whooped and grunted, drinking more and tearing at an animal they'd caught, the raw meat dripping blood into their beards as they ate. Crow threw some to us.

'What is it?' Ivy sniffed the meat.

'Sss ... some ... sss ... sort of deer ... I guess,' Sam slurred his words, but was still trying to be the animal expert.

'Who cares? I'm hungry,' I said ripping off chunks and sticking them into my mouth. It tasted better than smoked meat. Sam and Ivy took a few small bites.

The women had returned to pounding grain, as Demelza

had been doing. They mixed the pounded grain with water, moulded it into balls, and placed them on leaves to dry in the sun which became hot after the storm.

The rest of the day was a blur. We slept off the effects of their drink. On waking, the eating and drinking started again. One of the women brought us some more meat and some of the grain balls.

'Do we sleep in Crow's hut?' I looked down at Sam already lying on the ground.

'Dunno ... don't care,' Sam groaned. It might be his head that hurt but at least he had mostly recovered from the hornet stings.

Crow appeared and waved us into his hut. Animal skins had been left for us to sleep on. Demelza, already asleep, twitched violently in a dream as we entered.

Ivy hadn't been given the drink and had wandered around the camp. Now, she joined us making the hut crowded. Crow snored loudly in the night.

Next day, I woke through a haze of drink and sniffed. What's that ... stink? I sniffed again and screwed up my nose. I jolted, Crow's animal cloak was right up against my face with the eyes of the dead beast staring at me.

Crow must have left earlier and Ivy wasn't there either, but Demelza and Sam slept on. I left them sleeping and went looking for water. A group of male Stinkers sat in the mud circle and watched me come out of the hut. One of them handed me another skin bag, I'd expected it to contain more of their strong drink, but it was only water. I saw Ivy sitting with the women at the other side of the hut circle. I took a step towards her but she held up her hand and shook her head, it seemed to be an all woman group.

Even though the Stinkers were very smelly, that was nothing compared to the whiff I smelt walking out of the hut circle for a pee. Crow and several of the others were cutting up the remains of the mammoth with sharp stones. The tusks had been removed and set on one side. The belly of the huge beast had been cut open and its insides slopped like jelly on the grass. Flies gathered in swarms. I retched; Crow and the others grunted, almost laughed, at me before going back to their work.

The Stinkers were working away beside a small stream. I could see it ran off away down the side of the hill. A little distance away the hill dipped into a deep ravine and I could make out a bridge made of creepers. I walked over and looked down and saw a river at the bottom. Another group of Stinkers sat near to the bridge. They stood up as I walked towards them. I thought they might stop me if I went towards the bridge and I didn't think this was the right time to find out.

I went back and found Sam squatting on the ground trying to talk to Demelza. He had little effect. He kept calling her 'Demelza', but she didn't respond, so he gave up and 'Ass' became her name. When she did react, she would look at him for a few seconds and then look away. Nothing in her eyes suggested that she recognised any of us.

'I think she's in some sort of trance,' Sam said looking up.

'Probably something in the cave, watching what happened to Zach and the others.' I imagined the sights she might have seen. 'Maybe she saw them being eaten.'

Ivy appeared at the entrance to the hut. 'Perhaps we shouldn't talk about that for a while, at least not in front of her.'

'Do you think we're prisoners?' Sam asked.

'No idea,' I replied although I thought we might be. 'I'd like to know what's in that other hut.'

'I tried to walk towards it but the women stopped me,' said Ivy. 'They were quite worried and kept grunting something.'

'Well I guess the only way to find out is just to go for it, come on.' It seemed to me that we had to do something, waiting to find out might be a bad idea.

'But what if ...' stammered Sam.

'We'll find out. Won't we.' I set off. I heard a shout from behind and saw the two Stinkers by our hut jump up holding their clubs. I walked faster with Ivy and Sam lagging behind.

There was another shout. This time from Crow and the two guarding the hut moved aside. I peered in and at first saw nothing in the dark.

As my eyes adjusted to the dim light in the hut I saw someone sitting on the floor. I thought he was another one of the Stinkers – he looked and smelt like one.

I jumped when he looked up and in a croaky voice said: 'Hello. So she did come back. Thank heavens, now I can go.'

He looked the same sort of age as my dad and I thought he looked like someone dad did business with. Maybe it was the way he spoke but I didn't trust him.

'You'll like it here,' he said trying to hide a sneer.

Crow arrived at the entrance along with a crowd of the Stinkers. They pushed Sam and Ivy aside. Crow grunted some more words at the man who nodded and then the Stinkers disappeared leaving the four of us.

'Help me up.' The man held out his hand. 'My leg's not so good.'

I did as he asked, grasped his hand and pulled him to his

feet. He grimaced as he put weight on his left leg which was bent and deformed. I stared at it.

'Broke it. Slipped.' He didn't seem to want to explain.

'Who are you?' asked Ivy.

'You don't know?' He gave me a worried look. 'Let me get out into the sun.' And he started forward.

'Wait.' I held my hand up. He might be older than me but I wanted some answers. 'We're not going anywhere until you tell me who you are.'

'Is that right? Brave boy are you – think you can tell me what to do?' He looked as though he might hit me.

He definitely sounded like someone dad might have known but I'd learnt some things from my family and I wasn't going to let him frighten me. 'Tell me.'

'What does it matter who I am?'

'I think I can guess who you are, but I need to know,' I said.

'He even looks a bit similar,' added Ivy although with all the dirt I thought it hard to tell.

'Eh?' said Sam who appeared to have no idea what we were talking about.

'So?' the man said, tightly holding my arm. 'So, I'm David. Not that it matters. Who are you?'

'That would be David Tregarthur? You're Alice's brother.' Ivy didn't answer his question.

Ivy's words seemed to hit him. His head dropped and he slumped back to the floor. 'That's right. Where is she? She promised to come back for me along with ...' He stopped suddenly as though he had said too much.

'The full story,' I demanded, feeling stronger.

'Yeah, yeah. But I want to get out of this hut before I tell you.'

I helped him up again and we made our way out into the sun. David led us to a tree, slid down the trunk and rested his back against it. I thought he was deciding what to tell us. I really didn't trust him. Neither apparently did the Stinkers who had spread out around the camp and looked ready to stop any escape.

'What do you want to know?' David said eventually.

'Everything,' said Ivy firmly and I was glad she backed me up.

'And that means everything.' I tried to growl – like dad would have done. 'And not some made up story you've just invented.'

'You can't frighten me. School kids,' David replied. 'Don't even think that you can. Not with that lot around. They'll be all over you.' And he waved at the Stinkers. 'We're all friends here.'

'Just tell it,' Ivy said and placed her hand on my arm.

'First you have to tell me, is my sister here? They've found someone. Is that Alice?'

That didn't sound to me like the Stinkers were his friends.

Ivy started to say something but I stopped her. 'We're not saying anything until you tell us what happened.'

'That means it's not her.' David looked down at the ground. 'It's just you three useless kids. There's no hope for any of us now.'

He stopped and closed his eyes. I leant forward. I was close to hitting him. Maybe I'd learnt too much from my family, but I didn't care. Just because he was older didn't mean he could get away with lies.

The sun must have caught me when David looked up. There was some mixture of horror and sudden shock on his face. 'You're Theresa's boy aren't you?'

'What?' I stepped back.

'Same eyes. You must be Alvin.'

'What?' I said again, not getting my mind to work. The

teacher's words, her hanging around my house, her screams in the earthquake, my mother's face – it all whirled in my brain. 'What's Mum got to do with any of this? Is she here?'

I could see by the look on his face that she wasn't, but there was something more, something worse. 'Tell me. NOW.'

'Easy boy.' David shuffled his weight against the tree. 'It's far too long a story to tell you all of it now. My father has been coming here for ages, studying this lot.' He pointed towards Crow. 'Alice has been helping him. This time I came along too.'

'So you can get back. How?' interrupted Ivy.

I gave Ivy a nasty look. I needed to know about Mum.

'The tunnel, of course.' David looked puzzled.

'It's blocked, no way through, there was some sort of earthquake,' Ivy said.

David gave a forced laugh. 'Well that's sorted it, sorted it properly, we've all had it.'

'MUM?' I yelled.

'Bad news, really bad news.' The way David said it made me sure he wasn't going to tell the whole truth.

'Go on,' I said.

'You need to know about this from the beginning.' David wasn't looking at me as he spoke. 'Alice wanted to show me what they'd found here. It had been their secret for years. Anyway we came.'

'And ... Mum ... Theresa?' I wanted to know but I was scared of what he might say.

'I'd met her a while before. We were together.' He gave me a half guilty look. 'Living together. We came here together.'

'You're the bloke she ran off with?' I was angry but my voice broke. 'Ran off and left me.'

139

'No choice.'

'No choice!' I screamed. 'Dumping me. They're going to throw me out.'

My shout seemed to make the Stinkers restless.

David looked at me as though what he was saying was obvious. 'Like I said, no choice. You know what your crazy family would have done if we'd hung around.'

'But dad's in jail,' I choked on the words. I might not like what dad did but he was my dad. 'How could he do anything?'

'He'd have paid someone to do it. We had to run. Couldn't get much further away than here.' He tried to smile.

That made sense. My dad's so called business meant he had a lot of contacts. Even in jail it wouldn't have been difficult to pay someone to go looking for my mum and her bloke. But I wasn't going to tell David that he was right.

'Your mother was too scared,' David added as though that made it better.

'Where is she?' I said trying to keep my voice down. I didn't want the Stinkers to stop us talking. 'Is she dead or is that part of some lie you're making up?'

David didn't give a straight answer but he went on: 'We'd been here for a while. The plan was to use this tribe, show them to the world. It would make us famous. Alice was really taken with the idea. I couldn't see how it would work, neither could Theresa, we wanted to go back. Then the tribe got all funny about us leaving.' David stopped and I could hear sounds of the Stinkers closing in.

'Go on, quick.'

'Alice and my father escaped. Alice promised she'd get some help and come back to rescue me. That's about it. They've held me sort of captive ever since. I hurt my leg trying to escape.'

I could see that this was just a small part of it and David was hiding the rest. I had too many questions. Why hadn't he escaped with Alice? Why was Alice trying to escape anyway? And most of all, what about Mum? I wasn't convinced that anything he said was true. But at that moment Crow arrived with several of the Stinkers, grabbed David and marched him back to his hut.

'But Mum?' I shouted after him.

There was nothing I could do. Crow came back with a big grin and the Stinkers started grunting away to each other.

'The Stinkers do use some sort of words,' Ivy said. 'I think David Tregarthur understands them.'

'And he's lying about everything.' I tried to push against Crow but he wouldn't let me past. 'He's never going to tell me what happened to Mum.' I felt defeated.

I wasn't the only one who felt dismayed by what we'd heard.

'Will we ever get away? I think we've had it.' Sam's shoulders dropped and he turned, hiding his face from us.

We were half led and half pushed back over to Crow's hut. We didn't have any choice. After a while the Stinkers pulled us out and we joined the rest of them. More of the drink was passed around. Ivy was led away by the women and joined Demelza. Sam and I were surrounded by the Stinkers. Sam gave up and slowly collapsed and fell asleep after several more gulps of Stinker brew.

David was in his hut and well guarded. I tried several times to leave the group but they closed in on me. I needed to find out more from David. I had to find out what happened to Mum. Was she dead? But there had to be more. Was rescuing David all that Alice Tregarthur had promised? What was David hiding?

-13-

THE HUNT

We weren't going to find out the answers straight away. I wanted to get back to questioning David but the next day Crow pulled me and then Sam out of the hut and we found all the males gathered with clubs. Crow wasn't wearing his cloak.

'Hunting, I think,' I muttered.

'Hope so,' Sam said with a nervous glance.

'I expect they'll give us a bit of a start.'

Sam seemed to miss my joke.

Ivy poked her head out of the hut.

'Try and get some more out of David,' I called before Crow gave a grunted shout and they set off with their loping run. We had no choice but to follow, wedged in between more Stinkers. We were taken past the remains of the mammoth. Very few remains but still a lot of flies.

Then to the bridge. Crow sent two across at a time. I guessed the bridge wasn't strong enough to take the weight of more than two, but how did Crow know that? The bridge looked complicated, creepers strung in a pattern. More complicated than anything else the Stinkers had built. Who had made the bridge? It wasn't very wide but I could see that it saved a long struggle down the side of the ravine, across the river, and up the other side to wherever we were going. After crossing the bridge we soon came out of the forest to a wide grassy area. One huge tree stood in the middle.

'This is where we watched them chase the mammoth over the cliff.' Sam pointed to a dark green line that marked the edge of the plain in the distance.

'And that's where we stopped for the night.' I nodded towards the hill.

There seemed to be a track on our side, running up into the trees. Now I could see there were a range of hills leading to the mountains. 'That would have been a shorter route to the sniffer's cave, if we seen it,' I said.

'Oh good, shorter.' Sam didn't seem to want to know.

'It feels such a long time ago.' I thought of all the things that had happened since our first night after leaving Jenna and the others.

Several small herds of deer grazed on the plain and the hunt began. The Stinkers had two hunting methods. Either they tried to chase the deer over the cliff or they chased them and tried to hit them with their clubs. Both methods were exhausting and not very successful – the deer moved too quickly.

It was obvious that we were expected to join in. We could outrun any of the Stinkers, but were hopeless with the clubs, so we chased. Sam was better at this. He seemed to lose himself in the hunt. No trace of his hornet injuries. I think Ivy's leaves had saved his life.

The plain had looked flat, but dips and hollows filled with stunted trees and prickly bushes made chasing hazardous. I ran after a small deer, and fell headlong into a vicious thorny bush. The Stinkers howled with glee. The hunting provided as much entertainment as it did food. As I picked myself out of the bush

I noticed a strong stale rancid smell. I'd smelt it before, but I couldn't remember when or where. The painful thorns made me forget the smell. The hunt went on.

Lunch meant ripping apart one of the fresh deer.

'Are you going to eat that?' Sam gagged as I picked up a chunk of raw bleeding meat.

I shrugged and took a bite. Sam soon joined me.

By the end of the day we had five dead deer and one deer skin to take back to the camp. Crow threw the largest one over his shoulder and carried it with blood dripping down his back from the dead animal.

As we returned the sun started to sink behind the hills, shadows lengthening as the day cooled. It was very quiet.

Crow led the way, often looking back – pleased with himself. I was plodding on, still picking thorns out of my arms. We neared the forest. Too late, I remembered where I had first noticed that smell – in the sniffer's cave. I could smell it again. Almost at the same moment a shadowy form leapt from a deep hollow, shot past me and hurled itself straight at Crow and the dead deer on his back, smashing him to the ground. The beast was a smaller live version of Crow's cloak, but it still had long curved tusks and huge paws. It pinned Crow to the ground and tore at the deer. The other Stinkers ran away squealing, dropping deer and clubs.

Sam, nearest to Crow and the beast, grabbed one of the dropped clubs. Screaming and yelling he charged. The animal would never have seen anything like an angry Sam running at it with a club. It looked up and its yellow eyes glared at him. Sam didn't falter. The beast roared, its huge pointed teeth glinted in the last rays of the sun. Sam still didn't stop. He raised his club and screamed even louder. With more of a whimper than a roar, the animal turned and ran off. Sam still didn't stop and would have kept going if I hadn't sprinted after him and tackled him to the ground.

'Good move Sam but I'm not sure what you were going to do when you caught it,' I laughed and Sam joined in. Getting up from the thick grass, we found Crow uninjured, but frozen with fear.

I pulled him to his feet and Crow recovered, shouting: 'Haarfer! Haarfer!' this time he yelled at Sam, flinging his arms around him and dancing about. The other Stinkers slunk back, appearing amazed to see their leader still alive. I wondered how they'd managed to kill the other sniffer, they seemed so scared. How had they done it?

Crow made them carry Sam on their shoulders. I hoped this would change things and we'd get more chance to talk to David Tregarthur. Talk to him and find out the truth. But first this was going to be another drunken night after the hunt.

Much later Ivy told us she had discovered how they made the drink near to the dead mammoth remains. She saw them throw roots and plants into water filled pits and scoop out liquid a few days later. The pits bubbled with a thick scum on the surface. Sometimes the pits doubled as a toilet.

Before we joined the Stinkers, Ivy had time to talk. 'They didn't let me get near to David, but I think I've found out something. There aren't any children. I wondered if this was some temporary camp and they'd left the children somewhere else. I couldn't understand what they were saying to each other. The women seem to do a lot more talking than the men. I tried 'babies' but they went blank. I tried using my hands and pretended to cradle a baby. That started them off. All of them gaggling away. Then they started poking me and looking very excited. I think they thought I was telling them I was pregnant or something.'

'You're not?' gasped Sam.

'Of course not, you idiot.' Ivy looked at Sam and he reddened with a muttered, 'Sorry.'

'Anyway I managed to convince them that I wasn't pregnant and they all went quiet and started sobbing. I tried to find out more but they wouldn't say anything. Eventually one of them said 'Ass' and copied the baby cradling that I'd done. Then you lot arrived back all triumphant and the women disappeared quickly. There's something going on that I don't understand.'

'We need to get some answers from David,' I said. 'And now that Sam has saved their chief I guess we may have a better chance.'

I was right. Before the night's celebrations got started David was led from his hut and sat down next to me.

'All of it,' I pleaded. 'And quickly before they change their mind and put you back in your hut.'

It was much later before we made it back into Crow's hut and I was able to tell them what David had said. The Stinker party continued without us.

'David says that Crow thinks all male leaders who look like us are called Tregarthur – it just becomes Haarfer when he says it. Alice became Ass and that's what he calls Demelza.'

'So I'm an Ass too,' said Ivy.

'Guess so,' I said, not thinking. 'As we know, David's father has been coming here for ages. It's been his project, studying this tribe.'

'How did he come and go?' asked Sam spreading his hands.

'David said he used the tunnel but I'm not absolutely sure. What he said didn't sound right. I don't trust David at all, but I don't think he knows all the answers.'

'Stuck here forever then,' Ivy muttered in the dark and Sam slumped back onto his fur skin.

'What about the earthquake?' Sam sat up. 'What did he say about the earthquake?'

'David said he didn't know anything about earthquakes. He said there hadn't been one when he came through to this place. This was his first time. But it had been a while since his father had come here and I had a feeling that the tunnel isn't always open.'

'Did you believe him?' Ivy said.

'I just don't know.' I stopped for a minute. Wondering how much of the truth was still missing. I kept thinking about Mum. 'They met up with Crow and their dad was expecting all sorts of partying but everything seemed to have changed since he came here last. They were all miserable and fewer of them.'

'That explains it ...' Ivy trailed off. I stopped and looked at her. 'I'll tell you when you've finished,' she said.

'I didn't get much more from David before he was taken away again. He said the same thing he told us before, how Alice and his father escaped. He was left here with my mum and tried to escape as well but injured his leg.'

'What happened to your mother?'

'David says she fell over a cliff when they ran, but I don't even think that's the whole truth.' I thought that he'd probably abandoned Mum and tried to leave on his own. Something much worse than falling over something. Part of me didn't want to know. 'David said he'd get Crow to take me to the place where she was buried. It's a way from here, where they first camped.'

'That doesn't feel right,' Ivy said. 'That doesn't fit with her promise. How could she make a promise if they were running off? There are just too many questions.'

'We'll just have to try again tomorrow,' I said as Crow returned to the hut, crashed to the floor and started snoring almost immediately.

'Just one other thing,' I said in more of a whisper. 'David said he built the bridge. Apparently he's some sort of engineer. He said he built it and hoped they'd let him go. He sounded quite proud of himself for building it. I'm sure he is, but I'm also sure that he was lying.'

'I'm not going to say it,' Ivy whispered in return.

'What?' said Sam.

'We'll probably never know.' And Ivy had said it. 'But just back to the babies. I think that's the clue. That's something to do with why David is stuck here and something to do with the promise.'

'Go on.' I wanted the answers.

'I don't know any more. I need to ask David some more questions.'

Crow rolled over and growled. We stopped talking and tried to sleep.

-14-

THE PROMISE

Early next morning with grey light just starting to reach the huts, I woke to prodding and Crow pulled me out. No one else stirred. Crow motioned for me to be quiet, not by holding a finger to his lips but by clamping his hand across my mouth – effective if a bit brutal.

We headed off towards the mountains. I guessed we were heading for the grave, so David must have done something. I didn't know how I was going to deal with this. I was so angry with Mum for leaving, but I didn't want her to be dead.

Crow was almost at a run for nearly an hour and my breath came fast by the time we stopped to rest by a small stream. A few minutes later we were off again. I wondered how Crow managed to be so bright after partying last night.

Our route took us away from the heavily wooded area to the steeper mountain slopes and we entered a valley lined with huge black sharp pointed rocks; the shadowy shapes towered over us. The valley sides became steep and narrow, crowding in, the rocks above blocking out the light.

Then we arrived. It was just a mound, a pile of stones in a heap. Crow stood back leaving me beside the grave but I didn't know what to do. If Sara or one of the others had been there I guess they'd have tidied it up and found some flowers, made some sort of headstone. But this felt too unreal. For a start I didn't completely believe Mum was buried here. David could have lied about that as well. We weren't near any cliffs, she couldn't have fallen here. I didn't want to stay. I needed someone to be there with me. I wished Jenna had come; now I was all alone in this crazy place with some caveman who couldn't even talk. How could I make any sense of this?

I turned and saw Crow standing in front of an opening in the rocks. The way he was standing made me think he didn't want me to see something. I walked towards him. He held up his hands to stop me. Part of me wanted to attack him. What did it matter if he killed me now?

But I didn't attack. I just slid to the ground and the tears flowed. I couldn't hold it together. Tears and great heaving sobs. I felt this was the end. Even if we got out of here what would that mean? I had no life left, no family. I guessed Miss Tregarthur had been plotting to take me away.

This wasn't the brave leader I tried to become or someone from a drug dealing family of thugs. I was Alvin in a mess beside the supposed grave of my mum. Was I crying for Mum? It felt like I was crying for myself.

Crow clearly didn't know what to do. He was hopping from foot to foot. It was too strange, almost made me forget why I was so upset, but I looked at the grave and that started me off again. At one point he tried to pat my shoulder in a rough caveman sort of way. Then when he saw I wasn't stopping he tapped me again and pointed to the rocks. I think he'd decided to let me see what was in there in the hope I'd come round. So with a couple more awful sobs I wiped my face, stood and headed for yet another cave.

Light shone through a crack high above the entrance and a shaft of sunlight lit up one of the cave walls. In the light, I could see roughly drawn pictures. Fantastic scrawled outlines in red and yellow and black. Pictures of animals and people like Crow hunting them.

'Like something in a museum,' I must have muttered out loud. Crow grunted and rattled off something along with a lot of pointing and waved me closer.

Now I could see that many of the animals had been labelled in the same handwriting we'd seen in Alice Tregarthur's notebook. The writing was faded but I could still make out the names of the animals – sabre-tooth tiger, deer, mammoth. Underneath the names were a series of strange words that didn't make sense.

I tried to read: 'Gn ... aa ... cth.' The strange mixture of letters grated in my throat.

Crow gave a strangled shriek, fear showing in his face, and then he said something like 'Gnaarch,' almost as though the word was magical. I could see that each animal was labelled with something probably like the names Crow and his tribe used for them. I tried a few more, each time being slightly corrected by Crow. With each word Crow seemed to shrink as though I'd had found some strange power.

Then I saw something very different. On a ledge there was a plastic box. Something from a different time, a different world. I lent towards the box. Crow's arm reached out and held me back. I turned and saw that the caveman looked almost terrified. As though the box was dangerous. Crow's grunts sounded a warning but this time I shrugged him off. I guessed this was what Crow was meant to stop me seeing. I was sure this had something to do with David.

'I'm going to open it.' I knew Crow wouldn't understand but I said the words with as much force as I could. Crow stood back. I think I had frightened him by reading the animal names. I picked up the box. The plastic looked almost new, so out of place here.

Pulling off the lid I saw another notebook. Much bigger than the one I'd found with Mary. It seemed to be a sort of diary. I had to read it there. I tried, but Crow wouldn't let me take it away. It took ages. Then I needed to get back to Sam and Ivy, to tell them what was in the promise. And to do something about David.

Just before we left my eyes caught another cave drawing, not of any of the animals I'd seen here but of a small dog and labelled Smut without any translations. I said a silent thanks to the dog for his tin of food.

TRAPPED

Returning to the camp, David was the first person we saw, standing outside his hut. Crow grunted something quickly to him.

'What?' David shouted and he turned to me. He could see I knew everything. 'He shouldn't have shown you,' David stuttered. 'That cave, the plan. I know it looks bad but …'

I just stared back at him and was going to walk on past without speaking until David called out again: 'She did it for us. She's my sister. If you were older you'd have done the same.'

I walked on, still hearing David trying to make Alice's promise sound better. I was shaken by the suggestion that I might have done the same. I might never have been a good person but this was crazy.

Back in Crow's hut I tried to explain to Ivy and Sam. It was difficult because Crow kept barging in. David had obviously had a go at him and he was worried.

'Their dad, Mr Tregarthur, had been studying this lot. There's a whole journal in a plastic box near to a place David says is my mum's grave.'

'You don't sound as though you believe him,' said Ivy.

'I don't believe anything he says.' I suddenly found it hard to breathe, thinking about Mum and that awful grave. I didn't want to believe it was her. I felt Ivy put an arm round me but it took several more moments before I could go on. 'It gets worse – those Tregarthurs get much worse. When they came back this last time things weren't good. Crow had just taken over from the old chief, or probably Crow killed off the old chief – that's what was written in the journal. That's the way they decide on new chiefs apparently.'

'Probably what they're going to do with us,' Sam said miserably.

'No, I'm afraid it's not.'

'They want us for breeding, don't they?' Ivy had already worked this out. That seemed pretty clever to me. Ivy went on, 'There aren't any babies. It's something genetic. This is evolution.'

Sam looked mystified. I'd read some of what she meant in the journal but I didn't really follow it at the time.

'For goodness ...' Ivy gave an exasperated sigh. 'Don't you know anything? This tribe is dying out. They're some dead end evolutionary branch on the verge of extinction. That's what they need us for. Tregarthur's plan. New genetic material to rejuvenate them – keep the tribe alive. They'll want the others back at our cave as well.'

'Why did Tregarthur want to do that?' Sam asked.

I did know the answer to Sam's question. 'He saw this bringing him fame and money. He was going to go to the press and then run trips back here. He couldn't do it if there weren't any of Crow's lot alive. And he saw this as some sort of experiment. He had crazy ideas about breeding.'

'So what was Alice's promise?'

'She was just as bad as her father. This had been her dad's life work. She worshipped him. In his journal he wrote that he was getting sick. Alice promised to keep his work going, a sort of monument to him if he died. She saw that as more important than anything – much more important than sending a load of kids into slavery.'

'Worse than slavery.' Ivy's anger shone in her words. 'They wanted us as some sort of baby factory. I really don't like the way Crow's friends have been looking at me – they know all about this plan. And anyway why did Alice and her dad run off then? That doesn't make sense.'

'They didn't.' I went on, 'They were just going back for Alice to organise this trip. That was her promise, and she needed to get her dad home because of his illness. We knew that last bit already but David made up the rest.'

'So David didn't injure his leg trying to escape.' Sam still looked as though his world had ended.

'That must have happened before Alice left. You said her note promised to save David as well,' Ivy said. 'Maybe Alice couldn't get him back with a broken leg. She had all that equipment on the bus. Perhaps that was to help him.'

'I guess it's impossible to make sense of this. David just lies. He was definitely being held captive here,' I said rather slowly. 'Maybe he tried to take over from Crow and failed. But I think it's just too much of a coincidence that Mum died. Maybe she knew Alice would bring me here or even sent Alice to get me. Maybe she had a change of heart and ...'

Crow was back and jumping around. I thought he wanted us out of his hut but in a few minutes he was off again.

'We've got to get out of here and soon,' I muttered.

'What do we do about Demelza?' Sam looked towards where she sat outside another hut, still grinding away at a pile of grain.

'We have to take her with us,' Ivy said firmly.

'But she'll slow us up. She won't come. We can't ...' Sam sounded desperate.

'Ivy's right,' I said. 'No choice. We take her.'

It was then I realised David had been standing near to our hut, listening. Now he stepped inside.

'Bad plan. They will expect you to try and escape tonight,' David said with a smirk on his face.

I tensed.

'But did I hear right? You've got some more kids with you? Hand them over and we can all go home. They'll let us all go. I'm sure we can do something about the tunnel.'

It was too much for me. I shoved him. His leg gave way and he fell to the ground hitting his head on another of Demelza's pounding stones as he fell. I was ready for more if he got up.

'Alvin wait.' Ivy moved between us. 'He deserves it. Both him and his sister. But we need to know more. Why do they expect us to try and escape tonight?'

David rubbed his head and sneered, 'Well, you know about the plan for the Stinkers. You're not enough on your own, not enough children to keep them happy. But Ivy was right, they reckon you are near enough women so they're planning a big drunken party tonight in your honour and then ... well I'm sure you can imagine. They'll expect you to run when you think they're all drunk.'

'And us? Alvin and me?' asked Sam.

'You get killed when you try and escape. Simple really.'

'And how do you know all this?' I was ready to lash out again.

'They told me,' David said. 'I said we were all friends.'

'Or you told them. There's so much more you're not saying.'

156

Before I could get David to say any more, Crow and two Stinkers appeared. They picked him up and carried him away.

As he left David called out: 'Do what I told you, hand them over. I'll give you until tonight before I tell the tribe about the other kids with you.' He sounded as though he'd won.

The three of us watched him go.

'Why do you think David is going to wait before he tells Crow about the rest of our group?' Ivy said.

'He's probably already told them. He just lies and lies. I can't see what Mum would have seen in him.' I paced around the hut starting to really wind myself up. 'Actually I've no idea about Mum. What sort of person leaves her son and disappears? I'm going after David and I don't care what happens.'

'Wait Alvin.' Ivy held me. 'We've got to do something. It doesn't matter what David says.'

The hopeless feeling I'd had at the grave came back to me, draining the fight away. I tried to think.

'Do what?' Sam puffed. 'They'll kill us anyway. I wish I'd never saved that Crow.'

'Maybe not.' An idea was forming in my mind. 'They expect us to try and escape tonight. So we have to leave now. They won't expect that.'

'But they'll just see us.' Ivy sounded defeated. 'And what about Demelza?'

'We need to distract them.' I had an idea.

'Yeah, that'll be easy,' Sam muttered.

'It will,' I said leaning forward. 'You've still got Ryan's lighter?'

Sam fished it out. 'Here,' he said trying to hand it over.

'No. Sam I need you to start a fire. We can't do it here in

Crow's hut because it's too far away from the others to matter much. But that big hut over by the women, near Demelza, that's where they store their food and it's near the other huts. If we set light to that one it'll cause much more of a problem.'

'Can't you do it?' Sam was shaking.

'Not unless you think you can carry Demelza.' I looked at Sam who shook his head so I went on: 'When the fire gets going I grab Demelza and we all run to the bridge. When we've got over, we cut the ropes and that should give us enough time to get away.'

Both Ivy and Sam looked doubtful and scared.

'Ivy, it's the only idea I have. Unless you want to spend your life as Mrs Stinker mated up with Crow's best friend?'

Ivy shivered. 'But what about David? He won't fall for the diversion. He'll guess that it's us and he'll warn the rest.'

'I'll go and sort him.' I stood. 'We do it now, right now. Ivy, get over to Demelza. Sam you make sure you get the hut blazing. Ivy, try and tell Demelza what's going to happen. She might not understand but it could help. Take the backpacks – see if you can grab some food.'

Sam and Ivy didn't move.

'I'll join you as soon as I've made sure David isn't going to warn anybody.' I grabbed the other two, hauled them to their feet and pushed them out before striding off towards David's hut carrying one of Crow's clubs.

My plan started well. Arriving at David's hut, there were no Stinker guards. I thought they'd left to help the rest with the preparations for whatever was going to happen that night. My plan was to knock David unconscious to prevent him from doing anything while we tried to escape. I didn't care if I hit him too hard either.

But when I got to the hut David was fast asleep lying on an animal skin, snoring. I couldn't do it, not smash a club down on a sleeping man.

So I dropped the club and left. As I came out wisps of smoke were rising from the hut nearest to Demelza. I walked faster as I saw flames.

Then the wind picked up and the fire flared, sparks and burning leaves from the roof spreading to the other huts. The Stinkers started screaming and shouting, trying to move things from the nearby huts, some trying to beat out anything burning. Bashing at the flames with branches.

I ran to Demelza.

'She doesn't understand anything,' Ivy said. 'It's hopeless.'

I picked Demelza up, threw her over my shoulder and strode off towards the bridge. She started screaming and beating her fists against my back but the sound was hidden by the Stinkers' noise. Sam came out of another hut holding the lighter. We ran leaving the uproar. We hadn't been spotted.

Until David woke up.

Ivy and Sam had made it across the bridge and were waiting. Demelza's struggling had forced me to stop. But I was nearly there. Now I looked back. Thick smoke almost hid the camp. I could just see the Stinkers in the hazy gloom. They seemed to have given up, overtaken by the force of the flames, they stood and watched.

Until David appeared.

'They've escaped, they've escaped,' David screamed. 'Over there.' He pointed. 'Make for the bridge.'

The Stinkers might not have understood his words but his meaning was clear. Grabbing their clubs the Stinkers were after us. I saw David hobbling as fast as he could, slowed by his injured leg.

'Alvin,' Sam shouted from the other side of the bridge. But neither of them came back to help.

I looked down at Demelza. She was still howling and trying to crawl away. This time I didn't pause. I thumped my fist down on her head as hard as I could. She slumped. I grabbed her and picked my way across the swaying structure.

'Cut the creepers,' I called to Sam as I collapsed on the ground and saw the Stinkers coming out of the trees only a few yards from the start of David's bridge.

'What with?' Sam replied.

I realised the mistake. No knife. The creepers were too thick for us to break. There was no chance of escape. The Stinkers were coming with their clubs.

Apart from occasional grunts the Stinkers were silent, in hunting mode. David hadn't been able to keep up but I now heard his voice as he came into view. Other Stinkers passing him.

'Stop stop, no more than two on the bridge. Two at a time.' David was waving his arms and shouting again using some of the Stinker language.'

They took no notice and ran on. David yelled again. The Stinkers ran onto the bridge, moving much faster than we had. Hopping from each strand to another as they crossed the ravine. Too many, too heavy. They reached mid-point when the first creepers started to break. The bridge swung wildly. The Stinkers screamed again, trying to claw their way back. Then the whole structure fell. The screams died slowly as the bodies plummeted down to the river below.

'NO,' Ivy cried looking down at the awful mayhem. 'That wasn't meant to happen. They weren't meant to die.'

'We've got to leave,' I said trying not to look down at the pile of bodies. 'This only gives us a head start. The rest can still make it down to the river and up the other side. Come on.' I picked Demelza up again. But the other two hadn't moved. They were still looking back at the remaining Stinkers. Crow hadn't crossed the bridge. He'd probably understood David's calls. But now the Stinkers turned on David. He was still shouting away, saying that they should have listened to him. Some words in their language some of his own, a mixture. It all seemed to make it worse. I saw the first club strike David, then more.

'Come on,' I said urgently as I took off and now the other two followed.

Soon we came out of the trees and on to the plain where the hunt had taken place; where Sam had saved Crow from the sabre-tooth tiger. That hadn't seemed to help us, I thought, as I shifted Demelza's weight on my shoulder.

Demelza soon regained consciousness and it wasn't long before she started struggling again. We had to stop. Ivy tried to get Demelza to walk but she just sat on the ground.

'I'll just have to hit her again.' I looked around for something to use. My fist was still sore from the first blow.

Demelza cowered, she seemed to understand the threat.

'No. Let me try.' Sam took Demelza's hand and slowly pulled her up. They set off again with Sam dragging and Demelza reluctantly following. It was slow. Too slow. It wasn't long before

I looked back and saw some of the Stinkers in the distance. We were not even half way across the plain, half way to the path up to the hill. Taking the path was my plan.

'They've made it over the ravine,' I called. 'We have to move faster.' But now I knew we couldn't escape. The Stinkers would see which way we'd gone. It was an obvious route.

'We're not going to make it.' Sam stopped.

Demelza gave a frightened look. Now she started pulling Sam.

But it still wasn't fast enough. The Stinkers were catching us. Demelza collapsed to the ground, not moving.

'She's fainted. I think,' said Ivy. 'We've got no hope now. They'll kill us all. Look.' She pointed back at the pursuing group of Stinkers. They were closing on us.

I could see Crow and about six or seven others. Crow was still wearing his hideous cloak with the animal's head flopping from side to side as he ran. This group must be the fastest, but probably more would follow. I wasn't sure how many had survived.

'The tree,' Sam gasped.

We ran towards the solitary tree with me carrying Demelza again.

The huge trunk soon looming up at us.

The first branches were just out of reach. 'Up!' I shouted, leaning back against the trunk letting Sam and Ivy use my clasped hands as a step.

Demelza started to wake up. I wondered how I was going to get her into the tree. The screams of the chasing Stinkers seemed to bring her round. Before I could work out what to do she had scrambled over me and shot up into the higher branches. I needed to follow quickly, the screams were getting nearer.

I took a run and jumped for the lowest branch. I missed and

fell to the ground. The Stinkers were only yards away.

I ran again jumping as high as I could – feeling the arms of the Stinkers reaching for me. Sam grasped my hand while I grabbed a branch. We scrambled higher.

The Stinkers gathered together, howling at the base of the tree. Howling and waving.

'What are they going to do?' Sam whispered during a pause in the howling.

The Stinkers, being much shorter than us, were going to have difficulty climbing. But I started to break off a branch just in case we needed to fight them off, even though I knew it would be hopeless in the end. There were too many of them.

'Looks like they want us to come back with them.' And Ivy seemed right, the Stinkers didn't look as though they were going to attack us, they just waved and the howling started again. 'They still want us for their tribe,' Ivy spat her words out.

'We can't stay up here for ever,' Sam said a few minutes later as he peered over a branch at the Stinkers. 'I think they're getting fed up.'

His words were followed by the whiz of a rock thrown at us. I caught it and prepared to throw it back when I saw Crow knock the rock thrower over with his club.

'Crow seems to be stopping them from attacking us,' I said to the others. 'Perhaps Sam saving him is helping.'

'It's not working!' screamed Ivy as another stone hit her on the leg.

We saw Crow rushing about poking the other Stinkers with his club, but they weren't taking much notice. There seemed to be an argument. The Stinkers stopped throwing stones and gathered around Crow who was hopping up and down, grunting loudly. Then one of them came up behind him. I thought he might be the one who had worried Ivy – Crow's friend. That friendship wasn't going to last.

'Look out,' I shouted but it was too late. The caveman crashed his club down on to Crow's head. Crow fell to the ground and didn't move again.

The attacker grabbed the cloak from Crow and placed it over his own shoulders. Then waving his club he howled what sounded like a challenge and glowered at the other Stinkers. None of them moved and they all bowed their heads.

They'd found a new chief, I thought. Now we're in trouble. I was right. The stone throwing started again with much greater effort. Demelza yelped with pain as she was hit.

'We can't stay up here,' Sam said again, trying unsuccessfully to dodge the rocks.

'Just have to fight them,' I started to get down, ready to fight. We couldn't win but it would be better than being stoned to death.

But from near the base of the tree, in a bush covered hollow, came a growl. The small sabre-tooth tiger Sam chased had been a young animal, although I didn't say that to Sam. In the bushes near the base of the tree were the rest of the family. It seemed that the Stinkers had become a noisy threat.

The Stinkers tried to run as two huge animals sprang out followed by several smaller tigers. Running seemed to make it worse. The tigers' massive paws tore into the cavemen. The Stinkers didn't make it far across the plain. One animal caught the new leader on the run – the cloak seemed to draw the animals on, as though they wanted revenge for their lost relative. We watched as another Stinker was ripped apart. The massacre moved further away.

'Let's go – quick.' Ivy shuffled down the tree. We all followed. Even Demelza moved. She almost fell out of the tree in the hurry to escape.

I glanced down at the body of Crow. There was nothing we could do for him.

'Come on,' Sam called.

We ran, making for the track up the hill. I kept looking over my shoulder, but the animals had enough to do. Puffing and panting we scrambled up the track. I gave a vague thought wondering if this track had been made by the Stinkers or the animals.

No stopping and Demelza ran the fastest, the sight of the sabre-tooth tigers seemed to frighten her into action. We could still hear the screams below. Much later, we collapsed onto the grass, looking down on the plain. All was quiet now until a long howl pierced the silence, followed by an echoing answer.

'We've got to keep going.' I struggled to my feet and urged them on.

The path faded out when we reached the trees. On we went, slowing to a walk when we could run no further. Finally the trees parted.

'That's it.' Sam slumped down beside a stream. 'They can eat me if they want, I'm not going any further.'

I took one look back before I joined the others on the bank.

'I guess that's how evolution works,' Ivy said rubbing her bruises.

'Eh?' Sam asked and I was glad it was Sam who asked because I didn't know what Ivy meant either.

'Survival of the fittest. The Stinkers are dying out, no children and now the sabre-tooth tigers have hurried up the process.'

'That's awful,' Sam's hushed voice hung in the air.

'They'd have killed us,' I said.

'Killed you,' said Ivy. 'I think death might have been better than their plans for me and Demelza. I just don't understand why they thought it would work.'

Neither Sam nor I seemed to want to ask more questions about that, so we waited.

'Why could they think it was just the women's fault that there weren't any children.' Ivy huffed at our bewildered faces. 'It takes two to make a baby.'

'Oh,' was the best comment I could make. 'Anyway I guess that's the end of the promise.'

I looked around for somewhere to sleep. It wasn't just the end of the promise but the end of any chance of finding out what had really happened to my mum. Or of finding out how to get out of here.

-16-

BURIAL

'There's something we have to do.' Ivy stood in front of us. I rubbed my eyes, only just awake. I'd slept an exhausted sleep. I looked around. Demelza had crawled off and almost lay in the stream.

Sam sat up. 'Where are we?'

'The path didn't take us to the top of the hill,' replied Ivy. 'I've been looking around. We're back –'

'Oh no,' interrupted Sam standing up. 'We're back below the cave, the sniffer cave ... the bones ...' Sam groaned.

'Like I said, there's something we have to do.' Ivy's face set firm. 'We've got to go back to the cave and bury the bones.'

'But they're only bones,' Sam argued. 'It's ... that cave ...'

'We should have done it before.' Ivy turned to look up the hill.

'Demelza will go wild if we try and take her to that cave.' Sam pointed at her.

'Making her remember might wake her up.' I looked up the hill trying to see how far we needed to go.

'It might kill her,' Sam said.

'That might be better than being like a zombie,' I said and Ivy gave me a rather fierce look. 'Let's see how she is when we get there.' I tried to sound a bit more caring.

We set off.

'There may still be Stinkers about,' said Sam looking over his shoulder.

'I don't think that tribe is going to come after us now.' I didn't look back and we saw no sign of the Stinkers or sniffers or anything else.

The four of us trudged along the stream. Demelza stopped cooperating. For most of the way, Sam had to hold Demelza's hand and half drag her. She needed more dragging as we climbed. The sky clouded over and now, high up in the heavy damp air, the wind started to blow harder.

Sam turned to me. 'We're getting close to the cave and we'll have to spend the night somewhere. I don't think we can make Demelza sleep in there.'

But our chance to make any decision soon disappeared. A short distance from the cave the weather turned with a savage blast of wind. We were used to the sky suddenly turning black and drenching us with rain. We had to take cover fast and ran for the cave, even Demelza seeming to sense the urgency. The rain started. Then it started to hail; chunks of ice fell from the black sky whipped by gale force winds. We staggered into the dark silent cave.

Demelza's wail broke the silence with a scream a thousand times worse than the noises she had made in the camp. Her cry could be heard against the storm, it made me shiver and she wouldn't stop. I knew it was the cry of someone who had seen her companions eaten alive in the same cave.

I slapped her face. I'd heard that worked for people who got hysterical. It didn't stop her screaming. She hit me back and kept on howling.

'Stop!' shouted Sam and dragged her out into the storm.

The hail and rain seemed to calm her. She sat on the sodden grass shivering with water running down her face and she either slept or passed out. Sam and Ivy carried her limp body back into the cave and tried to dry her.

'At least the water has washed off some of the smell,' I said rubbing the side of my face where Demelza had caught me with her punch.

Ivy gave me a malicious look. The worst of the storm passed.

'Alright let's get on with it,' I said moving towards the back of the cave.

In the damp half-light, we gathered up all bones we thought were human.

'Seems so few to make a person.' I looked at the small pile, before we put them into the backpacks to carry. Leaving Sam with Demelza we left the cave.

'Can we dig a grave?' Ivy looked around the hillside. 'If we don't, then the bones are going to be found by other animals.'

'The ground is too hard.' I didn't want to spend the night digging in the rain. 'I think I saw a hole above the cave – can we use that?'

We carried the bones up the slope. Ivy tried to be gentle placing the remains into the hole but there were too many bone pieces and she gave up and just dropped them in, filling the top with stones and covering it over with soil and grass. On top of the grave I put the largest stone I could move. Ivy scratched their names on the rock using a piece of flint. Then we stood in the drizzling rain together, not knowing what to say. I was thinking about my mother and what might have really happened. Then we stumbled back down to the cave.

When we woke next day, Demelza was sitting on the grass. She seemed much the same, although perhaps her eyes were a little brighter. Setting off Sam didn't have to pull her arm so hard, even though she went at a slow pace.

Returning on the trail, with Demelza, took two more days. The route was less scary now we believed the sniffer had been killed but I felt relieved when I saw our waterfall and came to the river crossing point. The ledge had been blocked with branches and stones. It looked more secure than before, almost like the portcullis Stevie had suggested, but I thought Crow, or someone like him, would have been able to break through.

I blew several loud blasts on the whistle and waited.

Then we heard Matt's voice, 'Is that you Alvin?'

'No, it's the sniffer,' I shouted.

'Don't believe him. It's just us – we're home,' Sam said.

'Home?' I muttered the question quietly to myself.

Matt pulled on a creeper and the tangled mass of branches swung away leaving the ledge clear. We made our way across in silence. It hadn't been that long since we had left but it felt like months.

17

Re-united

I stepped off the ledge, climbed down from the tree trunk, stood on the river bank and the questions started.

'Where's Zach? ...' 'Is he dead? ...' 'Where are the others? ...'

Gasps met Demelza as Sam helped her down. 'What happened to her?' And when Demelza said nothing, 'Can she speak?'

I looked at them. They seemed so different from the group that had set out on the coach for a school hike. Being away made me notice the changes. Jenna, slimmer, looked good if a little wild and weird, as they all did. Cutting hair with flint knives was impossible, so everyone had long lank locks, washed only in the river. Jenna's hair, tied back, made her face much more noticeable and her eyes sparkled when I looked at her. Matt looked the wildest and had almost grown a full beard. Ryan, leaning against a tree, looked better but not recovered. Lisa held the hand of Zog, who seemed as shy as a human child. Mary and Jack sat on the river bank, looking pleased with themselves, probably wanting to show off their latest inventions.

Emma, Stevie and Sara stood at the back, slightly apart from Zoe who stared wide eyed at Demelza. Was she thinking it could have been her, if she'd gone with them on that night?

I saw the expectation in the eyes of the others as they waited for me to tell the story of our expedition. But I was leaving it to Ivy.

On the last night of the journey home, we stopped in the clearing next to the stream – the place Ivy had called the sniffer water-hole. We'd been living mostly off berries since our escape and I had gone looking to see if I could find anything else. I hadn't, and slumped down by the stream.

'What are we going to tell them?' Ivy said after a few minutes' silence.

'Go on.' I wasn't sure what Ivy was leading up to and Sam didn't say anything.

'Do we tell them all about Alice Tregarthur's promise?' Ivy didn't get a response, only puzzled looks. 'I mean it's a lot to take in, especially for the younger kids. Do you think they can take it?'

'No idea.' I picked up a stick and chucked it into the stream, watching it drift away. 'I suppose it's pretty dreadful, what that teacher had planned, but that's over. I don't think David survived so that's pretty much an end to the promise, isn't it?'

'They might still come after us.' Sam had looked back every few moments on the trek back. 'Mightn't they?'

'Don't think so.' I threw another stick. 'I don't think many of the men were left. A lot crashed into the river and the sniffers got the rest.'

'So do we have to tell them about the promise?' Ivy stared at me. 'Do we really want to tell them that they were going to be handed over to Crow's lot? Do we really want to tell them what would have happened? What they were going to have to go through?'

I knew Ivy had wound herself up about this. It was very personal, what might have happened. I remembered how scared she had been about Tregarthur's promise when she'd worked out what Crow's lot were going to want. But that didn't mean I knew what we should do, what we should say.

'I don't know Ivy,' I replied. 'I'd ask Jenna about it if I could. She'd be the best person to ask.'

'So let's just leave out the promise until we can talk to her and Mary. Don't tell the younger kids.'

'Do we tell them about David?' Sam asked.

'Couldn't we just tell them about the escape? Leave David and the promise out for the time being.'

'Fine. But you and Sam will have to do the talking,' I said ending the conversation. I was still wondering about my mum, there wasn't much I could tell anyone about what happened to her.

Not moving from the river bank, Ivy and Sam told our tale: of the sniffer cave, the Stinker huts, the hunting, the escape ...

'So you saved the chief from the tiger?' asked a wide-eyed Emma and Sam blushed.

'Why did they chase you if you had saved their chief?' Jenna looked to me rather than expecting a response from the other two. I turned so that only she could see my face and mouthed 'later'. Jenna nodded.

Ivy had seen our looks and rapidly went back to talking. 'And the drinking ...'

Sam tried to stop her, but Ivy insisted on describing the pit she'd found where the Stinkers made their brew and what else they used it for.

'You never told us that,' Sam objected.

They finished with the burial which produced a short silence before the questions started again.

'You're sure the other three are dead?' Mary asked and as I had expected Mary looked to me for an answer.

'Must be,' I replied, wondering how much to say about the bones. 'We found three skulls.' And I saw the shivers of those listening.

I exchanged the briefest of glances with Ivy. That glance carried thoughts we had never shared. One of the skulls had been a bit different from the others. We said nothing.

Ivy picked up the story again, 'We don't know what really happened, and Demelza's not talking, probably the Stinkers killed the beast and maybe saved her at the same time. We just found bones and a few bits of clothes and stuff, no other sign of the others.'

Sam looked at Ryan. 'We found your lighter in the cave.' Sam held it up as proof.

'Tell us about the blood again,' an excited Stevie asked, as he shuffled from foot to foot.

'And the mammoth ... and the party ... and ... and.'

The questions went on until: 'Hold it.' Emma moved to the front and held up her hands. Everyone looked at her. 'There's something you're not telling us.' She stared hard at Ivy who didn't say anything. 'Alvin, I saw that look you gave Jenna. There's something more and if I'm right then I guess it's to do with us, the younger ones. Miss Tregarthur was our teacher. You've found out something – tell us.'

I saw Jenna smile and I remembered her telling me about Sara's grave and how Emma had reacted. 'Alright,' I said. 'But it's pretty awful and ...'

'Alvin, no,' Ivy shouted.

'If it's that bad and you don't want to tell us then I bet it has to

174

be something to do with S-E-X,' she spelled out the word. 'But in case you forgot Mrs Wilks came to our school as well as yours.'

'Yes and she said we were better informed than most of you lot,' Sara added.

'So just tell us the whole story,' and Emma turned to me.

So I told them about the cave, about the notebook, the promise. I even put in the bit about my mum though I choked on that part of the story and Ivy helped me out. But I sort of skated over the reason why the tribe wanted more people.

'Babies,' Zoe called from the back of the group. 'This was some sort of weird genetic experiment wasn't it? They didn't just want us to be more children. If we were going to help them re-start their tribe then they were going to let us grow up and have their children. How could she do it? How could that teacher make this promise?'

'But why didn't they just bring older people? Why children?' Emma looked around for an answer.

'Easier to get us to do things, manipulate, make us like them I guess.' Even Stevie wanted to add something to the discussion.

'We'll never know,' Jenna added her piece. 'It could have been anything. But we'll never find out. But now we need to get back to the cave. Come on.'

We left the river bank, I still heard the muttering. I was relieved to see Jenna in charge. Jenna had been organising, including sorting out a sleeping area in the cave with separate piles of rushes covered with deer skins which made sleeping more comfortable.

As we arrived, Demelza seemed more confused than ever. Jenna pointed to one of the rush piles and Sam led her to it, passing close to Jenna who wrinkled her nose at the smell and whispered to me, 'Should have dunked her in the river.'

'She smelt worse when we found her.' I watched Demelza lie down on the bed.

'I wonder if she'll ever recover,' Sam said.

'If she recovers then she might remember things,' Jenna said. 'Things she would like to forget for ever.'

'She might have to remember how she got herself into the mess,' I added.

'Bit harsh,' Jenna said and prodded me. I smiled remembering her prods and punches.

Mary and Jack wanted to tell me all the things they had done. 'We've got much better at pottery.' Mary showed off some of the bowls they had made.

Lisa had let go of Zog who padded around, curious about everything. Mary tried to move their pots out of Zog's reach but Zog kept climbing up, grabbing for anything that looked interesting. Lisa led her away, distracting her with a few broken pieces of pot. Mothering Zog was a full time job.

'It wasn't just you two,' said Sara in a loud voice. 'We all joined in.'

'That's true,' Mary laughed. 'Everyone's been doing something. It helps to pass the time.'

I could see that the younger ones hadn't been particularly thrown by telling them the whole story. If anything it had been the older group who had looked most worried. Maybe they'd worked out, like Ivy, that they didn't need to get any older to be useful to the tribe.

'We've found lots more things to eat,' Emma said with a grin on her face. 'Jenna's been getting poor Matt to dig up roots all over the place.'

'And loads of nuts,' added Stevie.

Even as they talked about their new discoveries the questions still kept coming. I wandered out of the cave to make sure Sam and Ivy would give the answers. Looking back I heard:

'So you killed the tiger thing?' Stevie asked and stared at Sam with a mouth that had stayed open ever since we had returned.

'Not exactly ...' Sam tried to explain. I laughed as Sam's descriptions became more fantastic – with Sam as the hero.

I went to sit on the rocks. I didn't know until Jenna told me later that the rock I sat on had been named 'Alvin's rock' by everyone else. The late afternoon sun turned the sky orange and I looked down the slope to the forest below stretching to the river. I found the view reassuring; it had become familiar in a strange place.

'You found a way home then?' Jenna joined me.

'I think only Alice Tregarthur's dad really knew that ...'

'But he's gone,' interrupted Jenna. 'Mary and I have also kept something back. We discovered another grave by the river ...' she paused. '... near the cave where you found the old bones. Mary said she had a strange feeling there, so I went back with her and in the bushes we uncovered another grave and a cross with 'Dad' scratched on it.'

'I suppose we should have expected that from the note Alice left about going back alone.' I stared out over the trees. 'That means there's no one here who knows how to get back. But even if there was I think the earthquake changed things. David didn't know anything about earthquakes. He said they just used the tunnel. I should have got more information from him.'

'And your mum?' Jenna sounded unsure.

'Mum ...' Neither of us knew how to talk about this. I picked up a stone and hurled it as hard as I could down in the trees. 'Jen, I just don't know what to believe.'

'But the grave. Why would David invent that?'

'I don't know if he did. Maybe it's just that I don't want to believe it.'

Jenna changed the subject: 'So we're stuck. Do you think Crow's tribe will come after us here?'

'Don't think many of them survived. It was awful. I don't think Crow and the rest of them really understood what was happening. It had been fixed by the older Tregarthur and the previous chief. It was almost like it had become a religion. Crow treated the cave with the drawings like a church. And when I read the animal names out in his language he was more than amazed – I think he thought it was some kind of magic.'

'So we're safe?' Jenna didn't sound safe.

'Probably not. You think there's something else?'

'Yeah,' she said and seemed to hesitate. 'There must be other tribes. Ryan met up with one of them. I guess one of them will find us here eventually.'

'That's true. I see what you mean. They probably don't do neighbourly visits. It'll be just like the bad stuff back home. No one wants a visit from my family. What did Ivy say about evolution – the strongest win.'

'And I don't think they'll care too much about women's rights either,' Jen tried to laugh but I could see that it probably wasn't just Crow's lot who wanted some new breeding stock.

Jenna moved on. 'How long do you think David was here?'

'He said about a year. It must have been quite a long time because he wasn't wearing any of his own clothes, only caveman stuff and he looked pretty wild and rough.'

'So if no one knows how to get out of here what's going to become of us? Jenna prodded me again. I gave her a hug. I wasn't sure how things were between us – having spent time apart, but I soon found out. It was ages before I had enough air to speak. Then I caught a smell of roasting meat, my stomach rumbled and I got up.

'Don't know what we can do with Demelza,' Jenna said still sitting.

'I don't know how bad it was for her,' I said sniffing the air wanting to see what there was to eat.

'It might not only have been things she saw. You've no idea what happened in their camp.' Jenna stood. 'It's just one scary thing after another, but come on. At least you can think about it after eating some of our best food. The rest have been waiting to do this for you.'

She led me back to the cave and the fire. Matt had roasted a large lump of deer. We had more to catch up with. I saw how Jack had developed Sam's attempts at smoking meat; different roots had been discovered; stews had improved.

After a while Mary chipped in with her newest discovery. 'What do you think this is?' She held up what looked like a dirty lump of grease.

She received only rude answers. Mary took a burning stick from the fire; she lit her candle and showed off the blackening soot flame.

'We need to work on the soot,' she explained as she started coughing from the smoke and she blew it out. 'But at least it should give us some light at night if we want it.'

'I think if we melt the wax again then we can get out the bits from the fat. Cleaner fat should burn without making all that smoke,' Jack added. I could see they were a team. I think Jenna was happy about that.

In the dark of the night, with no lighted candle yet, most of the rest went to their separate bed areas, covering themselves in skins. Zog curled up next to Lisa. Sam and Ivy, exhausted from the journey, soon slept on their rush beds. I couldn't sleep. I could hear the others tossing and turning. What we had told them still fresh in their minds – worries that some of Crow's tribe might have survived and would come after us. I escaped to my rock, sitting with a faint light from the moon and a glow from the fire in the cave. My mind too full of questions to be able to sleep. Was there something we'd missed?

'Have you noticed anything?' Jenna said, joining me again and sounding as though she would give me something more to worry about.

'What? Apart from providing people for a new tribe even though we have our own Neanderthal baby in the cave? Then there's a crazy girl in the corner, the two inventors in love at the back of the cave and the fact that we seem to be a zillion years from home.' I paused. 'No I guess I hadn't noticed anything,' I laughed. 'But I suppose there's something worse?'

There was.

'It's getting colder. I think winter is coming.'

18

WINTER

'Winter?' I repeated. Winter to me meant Christmas. That time of family arguments when everyone came together and started shouting at each other, not that I had any family anymore.

'I don't know if I can cope with winter. What do I have to do?' I said suddenly very tired.

'Alvin ...' Jenna paused, seeming to search for the right words. 'You don't have to do anything, just be ... well ... just be Alvin.'

'Eh?'

Jenna tried to explain, 'The rest of them sort of do everything for you. When you were away they kept saying 'I hope Alvin likes this' with every new thing. Now you're back they feel safer – just look at them tomorrow.'

'Jenna, you're talking about me, Alvin. I only came on this trip to escape. Now you're telling me I'm some sort of saint?'

'No, but you're the only one who can do it.'

'How did it happen?' I was really puzzled.

'You were the only one who made decisions,' Jenna said.

'Jen,' I said. 'I can see through you. I know it was you that decided pretty much everything, you're still doing it, you're good at it. You've just set me up.'

'No I didn't,' Jenna said with not enough force, and then after a pause: 'Do you mind?' and she pulled me to her.

'Of course not. We wouldn't have survived without you.'

'But that doesn't mean they don't look up to you,' she said smiling and she punched my shoulder.

'Ow!'

I hadn't thought about winter. On our journey to the sniffer cave it had felt cold, but we had been high up in the mountains.

Jenna and the rest had time to see the changes happening around the cave.

'Sara was one of the first to notice the plants and the leaves were changing colour. Like autumn at home she said, but happening much faster,' Jenna told me. 'Even the days have become cooler and everyone has started to wrap themselves in deer skins at night. Jack puts more wood on the fire.'

'So what do I do about winter?'

'Say a few good things about what they do and it'll get sorted.' Jenna gave me another hug. We went into the cave. I'd forgotten how loudly Matt snored.

On the morning after our return I woke, late and quite comfortable on my pile of rushes with a deer skin blanket, and I heard and saw a scene of activity. Bizarrely, it reminded me of Crow's camp. I sat up and watched the others.

Mary and Ivy were using bone needles. Sara and Stevie had just returned to the cave and chattered away to Emma and Zoe, I heard them say: 'We've found some eggs!'

Demelza still looked zombie-like, but Zog had taken an interest in her and Lisa sat with them both, doing something I couldn't see. Maybe Jenna was right when she'd said they felt safer. Despite being stuck in this strange place they looked almost happy. Even Ryan seemed to have recovered a bit, although he spent most of his time alone.

All this activity was making me forget about Mum and the promise. I could see Jenna really was getting everything together. It needed doing. Could we survive a winter. Easy back home just to nip down to the shops, but here?

What was going on? Next to me, by the fire, Jack and Matt were chiselling at long thick pieces of wood. I sat up, puzzled.

'We found a better way to catch the deer ...' Jack started to explain.

'The bow and arrows didn't work?' I interrupted.

'Couldn't hit a thing,' Jack said.

'Me neither.' I thought about the small animals that had run out of the sniffer cave. Now I remembered that I'd left the bow in Crow's hut.

Jack went on, 'Anyway, we've found an easier way of catching them. There's a big hole on the other side of the river. We stick some sharp stakes at the bottom of the hole. Then we chase the deer into it. Not very nice, but it works.'

'The stakes have to be very sharp,' said Matt, testing the end with his finger.

'If you put them in the fire for a bit, then you can get a sharper point.' Jack showed me a dangerous looking blackened spike.

'Want to come with us?' said Matt, getting up.

'Us too.' Ivy and Sam appeared, sounding jealous that the hunting had been going quite well without them.

'Jack!' Mary said loudly.

So while we went on another deer hunt, Jack stayed with a list of tasks Mary had ready for him. Stevie caught us up at the waterfall and we crossed the river together. The barrier hadn't been replaced.

'Didn't think we needed to after you came back,' Matt said, sounding guilty.

I wondered if 'Saint Alvin' had to protect them by magic.

'We'd better put it back ...' I stopped, not wanting to say more.

'What, in case Crow's tribe come after us?' Matt did it for me.

There hadn't been any sign of the Stinkers, but Matt's words made crossing the river an anxious trip again. Matt led us to the hole and secured his newly sharpened stake.

When we got back I heard Mary's voice. 'It's just so difficult all the time. So many things to do – hunting, searching for food ... on and on ...'

Jack interrupted, 'We wouldn't keep doing those things unless Jenna kept us at it. I remember the days when someone said they couldn't be bothered and the feeling spread. She almost threw them out of the cave.'

'That's responsibility for you,' I said, finding Jenna who just snorted.

Mary hadn't been listening and had more tears in her eyes. 'We won't survive winter.'

'We certainly won't survive if all we do is stand around and blub.' Jenna made things happen. If anyone could make us survive winter then it was Jenna.

The colours of the leaves weren't the only change that happened as winter approached.

'The birds are going – each day the flock gets smaller,' Ivy and Sam reported returning from collecting chuckerns.

'Migration?' suggested Jack. 'Away from the cold?'

'I wonder what Crow's tribe did in winter.' My words seemed to scare everyone.

'Will they come after us?' someone said.

'I think we'd have seen them by now.' I often looked out over the river wondering who was out there. Part of me wanted to go back to the grave. To find out what? I didn't know. But if the weather got much worse it would be impossible to survive without shelter, we would be safer here in the cave.

'Maybe they used to go somewhere to avoid winter,' Stevie suggested.

'Perhaps ...' I stopped. 'But I don't think it would be any use us leaving here. When we went to the top of the mountain, we saw nothing but trees stretching for miles and miles. I don't think we could find anywhere better. Anyway, I still feel we should stay here in case something happens in the cave. Maybe someone will get through from the other side of the tunnel. That's obviously the only way back.'

'I agree. We'd get lost,' said Jenna. Then since we were all standing in silence and doing nothing, she turned to Ivy and Sam. 'But if the chuckerns are leaving, you two better catch some and see if we can keep them alive?'

'Yes Miss,' whispered Ivy as they left and Sam stifled a laugh.

Jenna carried on organising every day. 'Collect more wood ... catch more deer ... find more roots ... get on with you!'

If anyone complained she used my name: 'Alvin wants you to ... collect more wood ... catch more deer ...'

And they did it, while I watched and helped and sometimes went hunting. We added to the wood pile and started another pile in one of the other caves. Ivy and Sam caught chuckerns and brought them back alive. They'd tried to catch some of the birds that laid eggs. The egg-laying birds were further away from the main flock. Zach had missed them.

'He would have clubbed them all to death.' Sam's comment met silence as his words brought back memories of the death of Trog. I still wondered if killing Trog counted as murder, as Stevie had once asked. Zog grew bigger every day. She had never seemed to register her mother's death. What would she be like as she grew up? Would she ever be able to talk? Would she want to learn what happened to her mother?

Jack, Sara and Emma tried to make a cage for the chuckerns using branches and creepers but the chuckerns kept escaping. Eventually they worked out that if they tied their legs together the birds couldn't escape.

'You'll have to feed them,' Jenna pointed out.

So Ivy and Sam were sent to search the river bank to see what the birds ate and collected up armfuls of rushes, covered in seeds. Jenna said we needed more so they collected more. The birds went into another of the small caves.

Any fruit soon became rotten until Mary discovered it could be preserved by drying it in the sun or, as the sunlight became cooler, on stones heated in the fire.

'They taste quite good – a bit like raisins.' Jenna tried them. 'You three!' She stood over the three from the junior school. 'Get out and collect as much fruit as you can.'

'And nuts as well,' she shouted as they left. Jenna was getting fiercer.

'We are nuts,' Stevie shouted back, but they did what she said.

We caught and killed a few more deer to smoke. Jack and Sam had worked out an easier way to smoke meat. But the deer had started to leave and soon there were none on the plain.

'How about the fish?' I asked.

'Can't seem to catch them. We tried a spear but they're too fast. Might try using a bone hook.' Jack seemed to spend all his time thinking like this, planning new things to help us survive.

Jenna looked out of the cave. 'We need to cover the entrance, otherwise the rain and wind will get in. Matt! Where are you?'

Everyone helped Matt to tie branches together and cover them with deer hides.

Demelza stayed the same. Jenna put her back on pounding work. They'd found a lot more grain on the other side of the river. Demelza ground more each day, making a powdery flour. Mary stored the flour in her pottery jars.

One day, Lisa couldn't find Zog and searched everywhere before hearing her whimpering at the back of the cave. Zog had managed to slip into a hole behind a rock.

'Alvin, Matt – help!' Lisa cried out and we rushed over to her.

Jenna watched as we heaved at a large boulder trapping Zog in the hole.

'I didn't know that hole was there.' Jenna walked over and looked into the space that appeared after the rock had been moved. She threw in a small stone and after several seconds we heard the stone plop into water below.

'That's deep,' said Matt.

'Mmm ... deep,' replied Jenna before calling for help to screen off the hole as it became our indoor toilet.

It got cold, then it got colder, then it got much colder. For several days the cold kept us in the cave. Wind and chill rain blew in through our flimsy covering. I went with Matt to find more branches to cover the opening. We returned blue and shivering.

'We're using wood very fast. We'll need a lot more,' Jack said looking at the pile. 'How long do we think this will go on?'

'From the marks on the cave wall I think we've been here for about six months – that makes it November. If it's a normal winter then it will be three months at least,' Mary replied. She had taken over the daily wall scratching.

'Nothing's normal here,' said Ivy with a moan that sounded like the return of her miserable ways.

'Could be the Ice Age,' Jack said.

'How long does an Ice Age last?' asked Emma.

'About a thousand years I think,' said Jack.

Demelza became more distressed. She had nothing left to pound and she sat rocking backwards and forwards, moaning. It got on everyone's nerves. Perhaps Zoe felt guilty about the things that had happened when she had been part of Demelza's group and she tried to keep Demelza quiet. It didn't work and in the end Zoe got blamed.

'Can't you shut her up?' Ivy said loudly from her rush bed, unable to sleep because of the noise.

'Hit her over the head,' added Matt.

Zoe tried to hug Demelza, but wrinkled her nose because Demelza continued to smell like a rotten chuckern. The moaning didn't stop.

Some days were bright and cold and some just cold. On bright days, Jenna sent us off to get more wood. If the fire burnt down the cave became very cold, so the wood soon disappeared. All the chuckerns had died, but in the cold they didn't rot so quickly and eating them still seemed safe. I thought we might have eaten them even if they were rotten, although no one had forgotten Other-Sara and that terrible night.

It snowed. Not a lot of snow on the first night, but on the second it came half way up the cave entrance and on the third night, covered it completely. We woke up coughing in the smoke.

I tried to clear the snow. 'Matt, Jack, help!' I called, too weak from hunger to be able to do it on my own. The three of us dug at the snow with our hands and made a gap to let out the smoke before returning to the cave, cold and exhausted by the effort.

'Here, drink this.' Jenna gave us bowls of hot thin liquid from the stew. At least the melted snow provided water to drink.

Jenna kept everyone doing things, everything had to be done close to the fire. Mary and Jack still had some clay and still made bowls and jars and mugs. Jenna persuaded others to try to make things from the deer antlers. 'Spoons – maybe?' Jenna said. 'To eat the stew.' Because stew was all we had and it became thinner each day as we tried to save food.

Huddling by the fire, arguments started and scuffles became more frequent. The hours seemed to go by very slowly. Would anything change? Was this how it was going to be forever?

Stevie and Emma became ill and coughed a lot. Their coughs annoyed everyone. They developed a fever.

'Am I going to die – like Other-Sara?' Stevie's weak voice came from under the deer skin.

'Of course not.' Jenna gave him a bowl of liquid from the stew – her answer to any problem – her only answer.

Lisa tried to keep Zog away from them in case she caught their coughs.

'Can I help?' Matt had asked, but Lisa just raised her eyebrows at him. Matt was still trying to hang around her.

Because we had to leave a gap for the smoke, wind blew snow into the cave each night. Each day we tried to clear it out. The snow was winning. We were cold during the day and the night. Our stores of food would soon run out. Jenna made sure that no one took more than their share. Mary still ticked off the days.

One day Mary looked up from the marks. 'I think it's Christmas.'

There were tears as people thought about Christmas and families and home. Only Jenna and I weren't too upset.

Jenna told me that she had spent the last Christmas in casualty. Her mother told her that she had fallen down the stairs. 'It wasn't true,' Jenna added. 'Mum's boyfriend at the time liked to drink at Christmas, or pretty much any time actually.'

I thought there would never be another Christmas for me with any family.

'We need a Christmas meal,' Mary said, and she searched the cave and found very little food left.

'It's all rotten.' Ivy poked at the remains of the roots she'd collected.

'Chuckerns are as well.' Sam almost sat in the fire trying to keep warm. 'There's still some smoked meat.'

'Oh good.' I rubbed my hands together. 'Nothing better than charred meat for Christmas lunch.'

'I want turkey,' yelled Stevie and that started everyone off: 'Christmas pudding ...' 'Mince pies ...' 'Brussels sprouts – yuck ...'

'Have you got my present?' Jenna gave up searching for food and gave me a weak poke in the ribs.

I put my hand to my mouth. 'So sorry – I left it in the shop.'

'What was it?'

'Air freshener,' I replied. The indoor toilet might be a deep hole, but it still smelt.

So Christmas day passed in the same way as other hungry days. Two days later the snow stopped and wrapping a deer skin around myself I went with Matt and Sam to collect more wood. Outside the cave it was white everywhere, white as far as we could see.

I pulled the deer cloak tighter and pointed. 'The river has frozen. Even the waterfall has frozen.'

Despite the cold we struggled through the snow to look at the frozen river. The waterfall had become a sheet of icicles gleaming in the cold winter sun. We walked out onto the ice. Below us we saw frozen fish and tried to dig them out but gave up, unable to dig through the thick ice, and returned with the little wood we could find.

'We're not going to survive unless the weather gets better soon. We have to find some more food, but you can't find anything out in the snow.' I shared my fears with Jenna.

We weren't the only ones struggling in the cold of winter. Everywhere, life struggled to survive. I suppose animals were just moving around by instinct. Maybe some didn't get to their winter homes on time. That wouldn't have been a problem for us until ...

'Alvin ... Alvin.' Ryan shook me and whispered in a frightened voice.

'What?' I had been heavily asleep, exhausted and bad tempered with hunger.

'Sniffing – can't you hear it?'

I saw the terror in Ryan's eyes and sat up. Now everyone woke.

The sniffing had turned to scuffling and scuffling to growling. Sounds from an angry animal. Was our cave his winter home or was he just after food? He smashed through the flimsy covering with his front paws and stuck his head through the opening and growled – a deep growl that echoed in the shadows. Swiping away more branches the massive bear entered our cave.

I leapt to my feet, grabbed one of the sharpened stakes and ran at the bear. The bear swatted me away like a fly and I crashed to the side of the cave hitting my head and falling on top of Lisa. I lay dazed. Emma and Stevie screamed. The bear became wilder at the screams and reared up on its hind legs, ready to fall onto me and Lisa.

'NOT LISA!' Matt roared and snatching a second stake, he charged.

The bear, on its back legs, stood more than twice Matt's height and probably heavier than the rest of us put together; it turned to meet his charge. Matt stabbed the sharp stake towards the animal's belly. The bear smashed him across the cave with a single stroke of its giant paw.

I shook my head. Was this going to be the end, after all we had survived? I grabbed another stake and tried to attack. I was too weak; my feeble efforts only scratched the thick furry coat. The bear lunged forward and fell on top of me. I could smell its warm breath and see its eyes looking into mine as it snarled. I waited to die. But as the bear lunged forward, its own body weight must have driven the stake into its stomach, then upwards – piercing its heart. When I looked again, through half closed eyelids, the bear's eyes were dead eyes.

The cave remained silent as the others watched to see if the bear might come back to life. Jenna ran to me and made the rest drag the animal off to save me from being crushed. Lisa had rolled away and looked for Zog who had scampered to the back of the cave.

Then Jenna stood up with her hands on her hips. 'Right! Cut it up!' And we did, attacking the dead bear with flint knives, we soon had it skinned.

Sam made sure we removed all the guts. That was lucky because it didn't get cooked very well before our starving group ripped away the flesh and stuffed it into our mouths as fast as we could. There was still a lot of meat left even after we'd eaten as much as we could.

Mary saved some of the fat for more candles. 'Cleaner than the deer fat,' she said, as though, after butchering a bear, making candles from the fat had become quite a normal thing to spend the day doing.

'We've got to do more,' Jenna spoke to me after the bear feast. Nearly everyone else was asleep even though it was still early in the day – the food had made us all drowsy.

'Do what?' I was near the fire, full and sleepy as well.

'The bear won't last long. Eating it has given us a bit more strength. If we don't do something now then in a few days we'll be too weak again.'

That made sort of sense. I stood up and bellowed, 'RIGHT.' I had no idea what to do next but I was sure Jenna could sort it out and she did. She had us all working away – collecting wood, searching the caves for any chuckerns we'd missed.

'And Jack. Alvin saw frozen fish in the river. We need a way to get at them,' she said.

Jack soon found a way – putting burning wood on to the ice.

The ice melted into pools full of fish that couldn't escape. He and Sam found it easy to catch them after that.

Then Ivy came back having been searching for herbs and roots. 'We missed one of the caves. It's full of food. Most of it was to feed the chuckerns, but we can eat it. Some chuckerns as well – they're frozen stiff. We'll have to eat them.'

And so it went on, finding enough to survive – provided Jen made sure we shared it fairly, which she did. The weather started to warm again. It wasn't an ice age.

The bear didn't survive the winter, but as a dead animal it was enough to help us until the snow started to melt, the sun warmed us again and the animals returned.

-19-

SPRING

In the warmer weather we returned to the same routine as before. Food, wood and water. There was no change and no other options.

One day I watched Jack just outside the cave. Mary was with him. Neither of them moved for several minutes. They'd been watching the others finding things to do and Jack was staring at something he held in his hands. His face gave away his feelings.

'Jack?' Mary said gently. 'What's up?' She moved closer to him. I think they thought they were alone and I kept quiet. Jenna had found tasks for everyone else.

'I can't take this … what do we have to do?' I could hear the tears in Jack's voice and he didn't bother to wipe them away. 'I'm sitting here with a lump of stinking bear – can't even remember what bit – trying to make a bow string.'

'And?' Mary took his hand.

'That's it – nothing. Things just happen – winter, bears, cavemen. I … I … I just want to go home.' Jack's chest heaved. 'I don't want any more of it.' Jack threw the soggy mess of bear guts into the cave.

'Soap,' Mary said and she did brush the tears from her own eyes.

'Eh?'

'How do you make soap?'

'No idea and I don't much ...'

'Ok, you don't much care,' Mary interrupted. 'But you asked me what we have to do and that's the best I can come up with.'

'I meant what do we have to do to get out of here.'

'Of course you did and we all want to know the answer to that but ... when I'm cleaning up fat for candles it sometimes feels soapy. I think fat is only part of it. What do you think?'

'You must have to add something else and I don't know what.' Jack looked up and finally wiped his damp face.

I'm sure both Jack and I knew she was just trying to distract him, stop him thinking about home. Soap wouldn't have been anyone's first choice of a problem to solve. Although we were all dirty, we had become used to the smell. Hair remained a problem – Demelza's hair looked as though it had gone white, but the dirt made it difficult to tell.

The distraction worked for a while, but she didn't make him forget his thoughts of home for long. We all had thoughts like that. Later that day Jack came to talk to me.

'I've been looking at the tunnel.' Jack tapped me on the shoulder. 'Come and see.'

Jack had been doing more than looking. He had used a stone to scrape at the rocks that had filled the tunnel behind us after the earthquake.

'I think it's this big rock that's blocking most of the hole.' He pointed to the outline of one huge rock. It looked as though the other stones filling the tunnel rested on this boulder.

'You think we can move it?' I looked at the enormous piece of stone.

'I think we ought to try.' Jack traced his finger round the groove he had made. 'It's that or nothing – unless you have any other ideas?'

I didn't and I walked away in search of Jenna.

'Jack's been looking at the tunnel,' I said finding her slumped on the grass.

She looked up, questions in her eyes.

'He thinks we should try and dig out one of the rocks.'

'That doesn't look possible, does it?'

'No, but he wants to try.' I sat down beside her and we stared into the distance, the forest, the mountains.

'Being here does stop you thinking of stuff,' Jenna said after we had been sitting in silence.

'Stuff?'

'Home, step-dads, Mum, arguments – you know – stuff.'

'What? Easier than dealing with bears?' I said, but I didn't disagree.

'You know it might be easier – bears don't shout at you.'

'Just try to rip you apart. Yeah, much easier.'

'But at least we sort it out. I can't sort out anything at home.' Jenna had stopped with her face screwed up as though trying to make sense of how she felt. Then she continued: 'Here we have a pile of problems – hunting, finding food, everything. It's difficult but we do it – there's no one else to get in the way.'

Jenna knew she was speaking for me as well. No people to throw me out of this cave. She also knew I'd been thinking more and more about Mum, about what really happened. Was there more to find out?

Jack told the others about his idea. No one, apart from him, believed we had any chance of clearing the tunnel. The rocks were huge and crushed together. There was no trace of the hole through which we had come into this world. None of us believed Jack's plan would work.

'We need to scrape away at both sides of the big rock, and then see if we can get some creeper ropes around it.' Jack tried to make it sound possible.

'Then what?' Sam sounded as though he thought he might be expected to do most of the scraping.

'Then we try to haul it out.' Jack spread his arms out trying to show what would happen.

'The creepers will just break,' Ivy said.

'Not if we use lots of them.'

Jack went back to scraping and chipping. It wasn't going to be quick. He persuaded everyone to take a turn. Sam did his best to stay out of the way.

'Ash!' I saw Mary getting up from the fire and walking towards Jack.

He sat in the sun, rubbing his hands – sore after several hours of scraping. Days of scraping and chipping had done nothing except to reveal a little more of the outline of the main rock. It looked even bigger now. Occasionally Jack could get Stevie to help him, but the rest of us thought it a waste of time.

Jack's miserable state had made everyone, including Mary, fed up with him. Now Mary was looking pleased with herself. I couldn't see how Jack stayed miserable but he was still doing his best. Worse than Ivy, I thought.

'What?' Jack was staring at the ground.

Mary smiled at him, moved closer and brushed his face gently with her hand. I watched him pretend to shy away, but he couldn't resist and, while trying to look cross, he ended up smiling back at her.

She went on, 'I heated some candle fat in one of the bowls and it spilled into the ash from the fire. When I scooped it back into the bowl, it felt really soapy. You have to mix the fat with ash to make soap – look.'

In her other hand she held a squidgy mess.

'I should get back to the digging,' Jack said a few moments later.

'Give it a rest for a while. Help me make the soap better.'

Jack helped Mary. Without him, the work on the rock stopped. Everyone went back to making spoons and things from deer antlers or other useful tasks. Shoes had worn out and Ivy made moccasins. Using bone needles to poke through deer skin hurt her hands, but everyone wanted a pair because the thorns and spikes that fell from the trees made walking barefoot too painful.

Mary held the first soap up for everyone to see. It looked about as good as her first candle, but it worked and, although it did fall apart, it made soap suds in water and washing with it did get off some dirt. In summer, we had swum near the river bank or sat in the rock pools, but in winter, washing just meant a bit of splashing from time to time and not very often. Although the days were warmer now, the water in the river still ran cold.

'I want a hot bath,' Ivy whinged and Jenna told her to shut up, but it must have started Jack thinking as we found out later.

Jack had gone down to the river carrying a deer skin, down to the rock pools. Before winter, when they had been used nearly every day, Sara and Emma made a dam from a fallen tree trunk, making the pool deeper. When they lifted the tree trunk, the pool partly emptied, so it could be filled again with clean water. They were very proud of what they'd done.

Jack had built a fire and heated some large stones. Using the deer skin he dropped them into the pool. We all heard the noise the stones made as they cracked and sizzled.

Mary guessed what he was up to and she was the first there, followed by Ivy.

'He had to heat up a lot of stones before the water was hot enough for me,' Mary told us. 'Then we chased Jack away and jumped in with the soap.'

In the end we all took turns.

'When are you going to invent hair conditioner?' squealed Emma in the warm water while splashing her feet.

'In about a million years I think,' replied Mary.

-20-

INTO THE BLUE

Much later I sat by the river watching fish jumping and flies buzzing. I was thinking about my conversation with Jenna, about home. Then a different thought came to me and I turned to Jack. 'Did you see what happened to the hot stones?'

'They cracked and broke up when I chucked them into the water.'

I said nothing more. I knew Jack would get the point. He went very quiet and I could almost see his mind churning. The sounds of the others blurred into the background. Jack's fierce concentration took centre stage.

Slowly he turned to me. 'It might work. Won't be easy and I can't do this on my own, not like the scraping.'

'We'll all help.' I meant it, but somehow the words seemed too heavy for me to say.

'Before we get the rest let's give it a try.' Jack looked round. 'Mary,' he called.

The three of us tried to slip away back to the cave. Jenna still saw me and I asked her to keep everyone else down by the river while we tried something out. She nodded, but it was a worried look that passed between us.

We collected a pile of dry wood and lit a fire under the huge boulder – the one Jack had worked on for so many useless days.

Mary filled their largest pot with water. We stood back watching the flames grow hotter.

'More wood,' Jack cried and I ran off into the forest.

It took two more wood gathering trips before Jack was satisfied. The boulder glowed in the heat. I watched as Jack and Mary stood ready with the water pot.

'I can't go any closer,' Mary yelped as the flames almost licked at her feet.

'Now,' Jack shouted and together they threw the water onto the rock and dived backwards.

I ducked to the floor. The first crack sounded like gunfire, then the sound of snapping, breaking, and the rumble of falling stone. We ran. The cave filled with steam and ash from the fire.

'What's happened?' Jenna stood at the mouth of the cave surrounded by the others. They all knew we were up to something.

The air cleared and we ran back in. The fire smouldered on. Most of the water had landed on the burning wood. In the middle of the steaming wood lay a few broken fragments from the huge rock.

'Result.' Jack leapt into the air and hugged Mary.

I thought all the noise might have meant the rock had completely fallen apart, but it hadn't. Result sounded a bit too optimistic. But nothing was going to take anything away from Jack's celebration.

'Quick!' Mary turned to the others. 'Get more water ... and more wood.'

'Wait,' Jenna called. 'It's nearly dark. We can't do any more tonight. In the morning we'll all have to get wood. This is not going to be quick.'

Mary's face fell but Jenna was right. There was nothing else we could do that day. That didn't stop Jack and Mary almost sleeping under the overhang we'd made in the rock. They talked and planned. Nobody got much sleep. Anxious chatter filled the cave in the night. Talk of home. As though we'd already cleared the tunnel. It sounded too excited for me, too worrying and I wasn't sure why.

'Do you think they'll still be looking for us?' I heard someone say, I think it was probably Emma – one of the younger ones anyway. That made me think that they didn't seem younger now. We all seemed in this together. But were we all together? The talk moved backwards and forwards over the things that might have happened while we were away.

Jenna moved closer, restless and fidgeting like me, as though she almost read the trouble in my mind.

'Eh?' she said questioningly.

'Eh what?' I wasn't sure I wanted to answer. I wasn't sure I knew what my answer would be anyway.

'You've had some weird look on your face ever since the cracking rock.'

'So have you.' I would have stared into her eyes but I could only just see her shape in the dark. This conversation was going to have to go by instinct.

'Do you really think Jack can clear the tunnel?' Jenna said with a catch in her voice.

'Guess so, if we all help. It'll be slower than they want, but it can be done.'

'Then what?'

'We go home. I visit dad in jail then I find a squat on the street. I take up drug dealing, bit of enforcing. Might survive five or even ten years. Then it all crashes in on me. How about you?' I was almost spitting the words, but quietly. I only wanted Jenna to hear this – not the rest of them.

'Yeah. I guess I'll leave school and stay at home for a life long course in sex and domestic violence.'

'Sounds like a great advert.'

We both went quiet. Listening to the others. Their plans didn't sound like ours at all. That's when I knew we weren't all in this together.

Jack started organising as soon as there was enough light to see the trees.

'Make sure it's dry and dead,' he called sending off one group to get wood. 'No green stuff. The fire's got to be hot.'

The rest were sent to fill all the pots with water. We even filled the one remaining water bottle. One that we'd brought on the walk. Was that nearly a year ago, I wondered?

Rock breaking was slow. Sam and Ivy went off to get some chuckerns. Jenna helped to clean them. I was still on wood collection, having to go further and further. Matt and I dragged huge dead tree trunks from deep in the forest. Each time we got back to the cave there was another loud crack, more steam and a lot of shouting. But it was slow.

'We're going to run out of stuff to burn,' I said with a tired voice, sitting for a moment on my rock.

The last time I'd looked into the cave there seemed almost as many rocks as before. But Jack's burning enthusiasm didn't stop. He drove us on. He tried to get us to keep on through the night. Jenna stopped him. We were all exhausted.

Two more days and we'd maybe cleared six feet of tunnel. Everything was running out. Not just the burning wood. We were low on food. We needed a hunting trip to catch a deer.

Jack almost went berserk when Jenna suggested it. 'No. If we stop then we'll never do it. Who cares if you're hungry?' He glared round at us all before screaming. 'Don't you want to get home? Get on with it.'

But Sam and Ivy still went off over the river. I followed them for a while.

'So what's waiting for you back home?' I asked. I said my words without looking at either of them. I knew something was up because they hadn't been as excited as the others.

'Not much,' mumbled Sam.

Ivy said nothing at all. I left them as they scrambled over the tree, making for the deer on the other side of the river. I should have got on with the wood collection, but I sat a while and watched. Sam walked with his shoulders slumped as though carrying some heavy weight. Ivy looked about as miserable as only Ivy could. But at least we had some decent meat to eat, although Jack almost stopped us using the fire to cook it.

On the fourth day it happened. Jack had opened a hole under another enormous boulder. Bigger even than the first one. It was difficult to understand how it got there. Fallen from above somehow and stuck.

The fire was burning hotter than ever. Jack poked the blazing wood under the stone. He'd found a long length of bark from one of the dead trees and used it to channel water onto the rocks.

'It's like a roof gutter. We don't have to get so close. Means I can get the fire hotter,' he said proudly holding up his flaking piece of partly rotting bark.

I watched. It certainly was hot. Jack looked like a miner.

Covered in black soot. He wasn't going to stop for a hot bath now. He held up his bark gutter. Mary and Lisa poured on water from their pots. It formed a torrent washing down on to the huge rock. For less than a second it seemed as though nothing would happen.

Then a fissure cracked into the stone. It spread upwards. The stones started to shift. It seemed to happen so slowly, we watched – mesmerized as this beast of a rock started to split. A deep growling rumble came from above.

'Run!' I yelled, grabbed Jack and wrenched him towards the daylight.

Falling rocks and a cloud of black dust chased us. Spluttering and coughing we waited. The dust settled and we went back in. The huge stone had disintegrated, pulling down a mass of rubble but opening a gap into the tunnel. A dim blue light shone for an instant but another small rock fall blocked the view.

Now we didn't need the fire. When everything cooled down we could shift the piles of rock. There were still some larger boulders and we used Jack's first idea of dragging them with creepers. Slowly the path opened up in front of us. The blue light became stronger. The light looked unnatural and seemed to make the tunnel colder. We dragged rocks for another day but it felt that we were getting through.

Then, as Matt and I heaved and rolled another boulder away, the tunnel suddenly opened up – the way now clear. The way home lay before us.

It was time for me to stop. Jenna called me back out of the cave.

'What are you waiting for?' shouted Jack. 'Come on.'

But I wasn't following. I was standing outside the cave with

Jenna. She knew what was in my mind, what was in her own mind.

'What happens if we stay?' she asked after we'd been standing in silence while the rest of them slowly gathered round.

'You don't want to go back?' Mary sounded so surprised, hearing Jenna's words.

Neither of us replied.

'What happens if more of Crow's lot or some others come after you?' Mary sounded really angry. 'We've nearly starved to death, nearly been eaten by a bear. There's nothing here. Why would you want to stay?'

'Because there is nothing,' Jenna answered. 'Just us. I can't face going back.'

I thought of what lay on the other side of the tunnel. Why should I go back? I wanted to go to Mum's grave although I didn't believe she was in it. I needed to look at Alice's journal again if I could find it. But even if I didn't do that, then I wanted to stay here with Jen. She was right, this was our place to do whatever we wanted. Back home had nothing to offer.

Everyone else broke into anxious chatter. It wasn't only us who hesitated.

'What do we do about Zog?' asked Lisa, who had spent more time looking after her than working on the tunnel. 'I can't leave her alone here.'

'If you stay, then I'll stay,' said Matt but his voice trembled.

'No, I'm going to take her with me,' Lisa sounded determined.

'But Lisa, what ...' Mary started to give all the reasons why Zog would have problems back home.

'She's coming with me!' Lisa screamed as she held Zog tightly. Mary shrugged.

While the others talked, Jenna and I still stared at each other, then I took her hand, turned to the group and said, 'Whatever anyone else does – we're staying.'

'I'm staying too,' said Sam more firmly than he usually sounded.

I smiled. 'Thanks Sam, we need you.' I thought he probably said it because Jen and I were staying. But with no family left maybe he had good reasons not to go back. Life here had changed him. Had he changed for the better? Sam was looking in Ivy's direction. Now it made even more sense. He hoped she would stay. But Ivy didn't react. I think Sam was hoping that being firm might send a message to her. But Ivy had a home. Her mother might be a witch and sounded pretty crazy but it was home. Would she really want to stay here? It didn't look like it.

'I'm not going,' were the first words Demelza had said since her rescue. Nearly her only words before she said, 'And you can stop calling me Ass.' Demelza wandered off, preventing anyone trying to change her mind. Why would she want to stay?

'Well, I'm afraid I'm going,' said Jack, looking at Mary who took his hand, squeezed it, and said, 'Me too.'

'What, inventing soap not enough for you?' I said with a laugh, but I knew things would be difficult without them. 'And Mary said you had an idea for a water supply.'

Jack started, 'Yes, actually I've been thinking about that and …'

'Jack!' Mary interrupted. 'We have to hurry. I don't think the tunnel will stay open for long.'

Small stones had started to fall.

I could see that Mary and Jack felt guilty about leaving, but neither of them would want to spend the rest of their lives in this weird world.

'Sorry … about the water supply,' Jack muttered.

'Maybe next time,' I said with a grin. Jack nodded, but jolted when he realised what I had said.

'The rest of you are coming with me whether you like it or not. I don't want us to be the only ones trying to explain all this,' Mary said loudly. Then she came and wrapped her arms around me.

'You've done it Alvin. If it hadn't been for you,' she loosened her hold and turned. 'And you Jen. If it hadn't been for you two we would all be dead.'

Jenna gave her a look which I thought meant thanks and you can let go of him now.

'You and Jack did it too,' I said rather quickly.

'Maybe, but no one would have expected you to make it happen. You're Alvin Carter. Didn't know you had saviour written on your heart.'

I was now a beetroot red. Jenna untangled Mary from me and took her place. 'And he's my Alvin Carter now, so you can't go wandering off up the mountain with him.' They both smiled at each other in a fairly friendly way. I think I found a colour redder than beetroot – not that I know much about vegetables.

Goodbyes were short; it looked as though the tunnel could be blocked off again by another rock fall at any minute.

Emma hesitated in the tunnel, ran back and gave me a kiss saying, 'Thanks.' before she ran after the rest of them.

Jack led the way.

We shouted, 'Good luck!' Demelza returned to the cave, peered at the leaving group and seemed to wave.

Lisa carried Zog towards the blue light. Zog went wild, screeching, scratching and biting as Lisa tried to enter the tunnel. She came back, talking to Zog. Back in the cave, Zog calmed down immediately and snuggled into Lisa. She tried again. This time it was worse.

'She won't go.' Lisa's eyes were red with tears as she turned to Jenna. Lisa tried again, cuddling and stroking Zog as she walked towards the others. The same thing happened – it wasn't going to work.

'Lisa – come on, the rocks are falling!' Jack shouted as the ground start to shake. 'It's the earthquake ...' his voice drowned by falling stone.

Lisa sank to the floor, her face red and bloated from crying. Jenna took a step towards her. I stretched out my arm to stop her. 'She has to decide.'

Appearing like a ghost through the dust and noise, Ivy came striding back.

'Here.' Ivy took the struggling Zog from Lisa. 'Now GO!' And Ivy pulled Lisa to her feet and pushed her into the tunnel. Lisa stumbled on with no chance to look back as the passage disappeared in one last fall of rocks. The tunnel roof had caved in, no chance of breaking through again, no way to follow them now.

'That's it then.' Jenna turned away and looked out of the cave.

Sam looked as though everything wonderful that could happen had arrived in that moment Ivy came back. But he couldn't find any words. He just beamed at her.

We stood in silence until Ivy said in a cheerful voice, 'What's for dinner?' and put Zog down, who scampered off.

'Oh – a special stew I expect,' Jenna tried to smile.

'Not chuckern again?' Ivy's rare grins were always worth waiting for.

'Now and forever,' I said and I walked back out to my rock.

JACK'S NOTE

———————————

Alvin asked me to make sure I wrote it all down. Everything that happened when we got back. Just in case we should ever meet again.

We ran through the tunnel. I wasn't going to be slow like last time. As we went through a thick blue mist seemed to stick to us. All traces of the time we had spent together started to disappear. Mary's candle evaporated leaving her stumbling in the gloom. The deer hide clothes and shoes, which had taken so long to make, started to fall apart leaving some of us almost naked.

We stumbled on, back into the earthquake. Lisa did stop and tried to turn back, but Matt grabbed her and pulled her onwards.

Then we were out on the other side. Different blue lights flashed in all directions, their hazy light giving an eerie glow. Sirens wailed and I heard loud shouts. There was a full moorland rescue going on. Not that they had found us. As we looked back, all sign of the tunnel vanished in the mist.

We were grabbed by the rescue team and there were masses of questions. Lots of parents had turned up along with the TV. It was mayhem. Helicopters whirred in the distance. They wrapped us in foil blankets and gave us hot drinks.

I remember asking how long they had been searching for us.

'All day, love, searching all day,' had replied a lady handing out tea.

I thought that couldn't be right. Hadn't we been away for nearly a year? Now it seemed as though this was the same day we had started the walk. We'd only been missing for a few hours not months. Time seemed to have changed in the tunnel.

Police came with clipboards. Everyone talked at once, asking the same questions: 'What happened?', 'Where are the rest of you?' as it became obvious that not everyone had been found.

So we told them and of course no one believed a word. They thought we'd invented it – some sort of stupid game. People got really angry.

Miss Tregarthur had been found unconscious. She had been hit by a boulder and whisked off in an ambulance. None of the other walkers had been harmed. It seems a lot of them hadn't got far enough up the hill to be hit by the earthquake.

We were moved on. Transported to hospital and examined but despite the cuts and grazes from the tunnel no one needed to be kept in for treatment.

More questions followed, not all the police questions were friendly. Eventually we were taken home. The television carried news bulletins from serious looking people talking of terrible events. The newspapers said something had to be done. The news story went on for weeks. Searching went on for months. The earthquake and the mist on a treacherous moor were the only explanations. But no one took any notice of our story and the tunnel.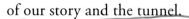

In time, our life returned to its normal pattern. Slowly I stopped being able to remember what had happened. Small fragments sometimes returned in flashbacks. But brief flashbacks were all I had. Mary and I stuck together.

School started again after the summer holidays. Our friends seemed to think we were strange. From time to time people asked more questions. TV and newspaper reporters often wanted stories. Christmas came and I had strange dreams.

One night I lay in bed. Then I heard sniffing. I felt a cold shiver running up my spine. The door pushed opened, and my dog bounded in and jumped onto my bed. I was just sure that it had been a huge bear pushing at my door.

MISS TREGARTHUR

(EPILOGUE)

'Jack, we should go and see her,' said Mary.

We were walking home from school and I knew she meant Miss Tregarthur. It was almost one year since the moor walk.

Miss Tregarthur had not recovered and had been moved to a nursing home in the West of England. We had to wait several days before we could get away unnoticed. We took the train and walked from the station to the nursing home.

'Can we see her?' and Mary explained who we were to the nursing staff.

'Of course, you can,' said the nurse. 'But don't expect anything – she doesn't speak at all.'

We went up to Miss Tregarthur's room.

'Don't worry about Smut,' the nurse called as I opened the door, wondering what she meant.

Miss Tregarthur, bed ridden, lay with eyes closed with an ancient mongrel asleep in a basket on the floor.

'Miss Tregarthur,' Mary said from the bedside. 'It's Mary and

Jack from the school. We want to find out what happened on the moor.' No response. 'We want to know why you wanted to take us there. Why did you do it?' Mary sounded angry. 'I don't think we're going to get any sense from her.'

'He's dead, your brother's dead,' I blurted out.

Silence. Then Alice Tregarthur's eyes snapped open. She raised her head, fixed me with a stare and said in a trembling voice, 'Why did you come back? You weren't meant to come back.' She collapsed back onto the pillows, and seemed unconscious.

Smut growled and we prepared to leave. As we opened the door Miss Tregarthur's voice rang out one last time, stronger now: 'Go and look under the stone. Then you'll see. It'll never end.'

Very early one morning we travelled to the moor.

'We go that way,' Mary said, looking up from the map she had brought with us. 'Along the stream in the valley. I think we stopped for lunch somewhere near a bridge.'

'Can you see the hill from here?' I looked over her shoulder. 'All I seem to remember was a lot of mud.'

'I think that black mound is where we have to make for.' Mary pointed again.

The sun shone as it had done at the start of the previous expedition. This time we reached the summit of the hill.

'Looks like it's going to fall.' I pointed at a granite rock that looked dangerously balanced on another.

'I don't think so,' said Mary. 'It's been like this for thousands of years.'

'What are we looking for?' I said as Mary searched around the stones.

'No idea.' Mary turned her head, staring past the hanging

stones. 'But I've done this before.'

We searched and found nothing. We started to leave. Then Mary saw another stone nearby.

'Wait,' she said as though a memory suddenly came back to her. 'Dog food,' she muttered, rolling the stone over and scrabbling in the ground underneath.

A little later, with hands black from the peaty soil, she held up a small package wrapped in something that looked like very old leather – or deer skin – and crumbled to dust, leaving Mary holding a flat piece of stone.

'It's a message ...' she said peering at deep scratches on the stone, '... from Jenna.'

I leant over her. 'But she's still back there isn't she ... how ... what does it say?

'Help – come back – Zach's not dead.'

- END OF BOOK I -

ABOUT THE AUTHOR

This is ALEX MELLANBY's first novel, although not his first work of fiction since, as a doctor, he has had many research papers published. Unable to stick general practice, psychiatry or even being a physician, he took up a senior post in Public Health - which mostly involved drain sniffing. He was brought back to sanity with an MA course in creative writing at the Anglia Ruskin University, Cambridge. Inspired whilst living in Devon, Alex is writing the Tregarthur's series, following his characters through some of the worst of possible and impossible times.

www.tregarthurseries.com

Join in on the conversation at
facebook.com/tregarthurseries

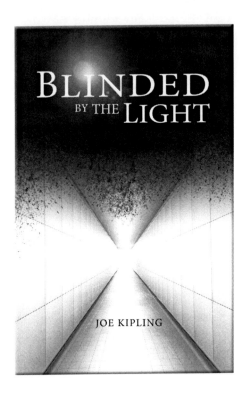

BLINDED
BY THE LIGHT

JOE KIPLING

Also by Cillian Press

The Union Trilogy - Book 1

In the future, when the world's population has been decimated by disease, the fortunate few live inside the Boundary, while the unlucky ones are left to die on the Outside. MaryAnn is one of the privileged. It doesn't matter that her friends can sometimes be cruel or that the boy she likes just threw up on her shoes, it's all about being noticed at the right parties.

But it takes a single event to rip her life apart.

Blinded by the Light
by Joe Kipling

Lightning Source UK Ltd.
Milton Keynes UK
UKOW03f1915100414

229784UK00003B/82/P